# ENEMY

## THE MALICHEA QUEST

# THE LAST ENEMY

## THE MALICHEA QUEST

# JIM ELDRIDGE

### BLOOMSBURY

LONDON   NEW DELHI   NEW YORK   SYDNEY

Bloomsbury Publishing, London, New Delhi, New York and Sydney

First published in Great Britain in September 2013 by
Bloomsbury Publishing Plc
50 Bedford Square, London WC1B 3DP

A CIP catalogue record for this book is available from the British Library

ISBN 978 1 4088 1722 3

Typeset by Hewer Text UK Ltd, Edinburgh
Printed and bound in Great Britain by CPI Group (UK) Ltd, Croydon CR0 4YY

1 3 5 7 9 10 8 6 4 2

www.bloomsbury.com
www.jimeldridge.com

To Lynne, as ever, for ever, my inspiration

Alex Munro, CEO of Pierce Randall, got out of his chauffeur-driven car and looked along Crouch End Broadway, his eye lighting on the Red Hen Café just five paces away from where he stood. It was very rare that a man in his position, one of the most powerful lawyers in the world, made a personal 'home visit'. People came to see *him*, not the other way around. But this was a special case. The person he'd come here to meet could well be the way into the mother-lode; the key to the whole hidden library of the Order of Malichea. If it turned out to be so, then this could signal millions — no, *billions* of dollars coming in to the company for ever.

His driver, Arnold, closed the rear passenger door and shot Munro a questioning look that asked: do you need me with you? Munro shook his head. No, he didn't need Arnold with him, everything seemed safe. He'd got his security people to check out the Red Hen Café;

the owners, the clientele. Five of his bodyguards, all ex-military, were inside the small café posing as customers and ready to spring into action if needed. If there was going to be any hint of trouble they'd have sorted that out already, before Munro even entered the place.

He looked at his watch, and checked it with the giant clock on the imposing brick monument in the centre of the Broadway. 2 p.m. That was the time agreed. He wondered if the person he was due to meet was already inside the café, waiting for him; or whether they'd be late? He hoped they'd be on time; he couldn't stand unpunctuality.

He nodded at Arnold, who got back into the car. Then Munro moved across the pavement towards the café.

He never made it.

As he took his second step, the bullet smashed into the back of his head and ripped through his brain, sending blood erupting out from the exit wound. He was dead before he hit the ground.

The figure high up on the roof of the old building overlooking the Broadway began to take apart the sniper rifle and put it into its case. When he reappeared on the street below in a few moments, he would just be carrying an ordinary attaché case. He'd disappear into the crowd, just a regular person going about his business.

The first part of The Plan had been carried out. Alex Munro was dead. Now to concentrate on his next target: Jake Wells.

# Chapter 1

Jake Wells still wasn't sure if it had been a genuine meeting that had been abandoned at the last minute, or someone playing a trick on him.

'Someone wants to meet you,' the voice on the phone had told him earlier that morning. 'They have information about The Index.'

The Index. The Holy Grail for people who were hunting for the hidden books of the Order of Malichea. The list of where each individual book was hidden.

'Who?' Jake had asked.

'No names,' the voice had said. 'Be at Muswell Hill Broadway at half past one today. Come alone. They will recognise you.'

And so, at 1.20 p.m., Jake had been at Muswell Hill Broadway, standing in plain sight so that he could be easily spotted. By 1.40 p.m., he was still standing at the same spot, alone and uncontacted.

Then, at 1.45 p.m., he'd got a text. 'Meeting off. In touch later.'

And that was it.

He'd driven back to his and Lauren's flat in Finsbury Park, all the way still not sure whether it had been a stitch-up from the start, or if the mysterious person had been genuine but had really been forced to cancel at the last minute and would, as they had promised, be 'in touch later'. As he drove he reflected on how their lives had changed in the six months since Lauren had returned to England. Before, they'd been separated by a whole planet, with Lauren in New Zealand. Now they had a flat of their own, in London, and even a car. And not just a car but Jake's dream car, a Mini Cooper.

He parked the Mini in the small car park at their block of flats and wondered what to do. He wanted to phone Lauren and tell her what had happened, how it had been a no-show, but she'd told him it was all too simple, that it was highly unlikely that someone would suddenly appear with information that would lead them to The Index. She'd said it would be a set-up, and now he'd have to tell her she'd been right and he'd been wrong. Not that she'd gloat about it, Lauren wasn't that kind of person, but there'd be just a little hint of smugness about her when he told her, and that would irritate him.

He sat in the car and weighed up his options. He could wait for Lauren to return from the British Library and then tell her his meeting at Muswell Hill had been a waste of time; but he knew she wouldn't be back till late in the afternoon. Or he could go to the British Library now and meet her, get his pride dented quickly and over with.

OK, he told himself. The British Library it is.

As Jake stood on the platform at Finsbury Park tube station he could swear that he was being watched. It was strange; there was no logical reason for the feeling, but his experiences over the past eighteen months had shown him that he had entered a world where *everyone* was suspect: so many of the people he'd encountered since he'd started hunting for the hidden books of Malichea hadn't been what they had seemed to be at first. Harmless-looking people had turned out to be ruthless killers. Apparent villains had turned out to be good guys. And they were just the ones he'd actually encountered. He knew there had to be many more people who'd stayed firmly in the shadows and pulled the strings behind the scenes.

Like now. As he waited for the next train — due in two minutes, according to the display board — a sixth sense he'd developed told him that someone's eyes were on him. Not just a casual observer, but concentrated on him. When all this had first started, someone had tried to push him to his death under a tube train at Victoria Station. Whenever things got bad, he could still feel the force of that unknown hand against his back, feel himself falling forwards . . .

He looked along the platform. There were about thirty or forty people waiting with him: a mixture of all ages, men and women, young and old, different dress styles. No one stood out.

But that was how they operated, he'd learnt to his cost. People who looked ordinary, nothing special, nothing to attract attention, but who were part of a massive conspiracy to obtain the hidden books of Malichea. People who would do anything to get their hands on them, and especially The Index. People who would kill.

He moved back from his position near the edge of the platform. It wasn't at all crowded, but Jake was taking no chances.

The train came in and Jake got on board, scrutinising the people who came into the carriage with him. An elderly Asian woman with a shopping bag on wheels. A young black guy, dressed in a smart business suit, wearing headphones, from which Jake could vaguely hear classical music. A pair of teenage girls, chattering away excitedly to one another. An older white guy, shaven-headed and covered with tattoos, who had a deep scowl on his face.

Was the person watching him one of them, wondered Jake. Or had they got into an adjoining carriage, where

6

they could watch him without being observed, and just get off when he did? Or was there even anyone watching him at all? Had his terrifying experiences with the search for the Malichea books made him paranoid?

He got off at King's Cross. None of the people who'd entered the same carriage as him at Finsbury Park exited with him. But then, that didn't mean they weren't watching him. The young black guy could be passing messages on to another watcher via his headphones. Modern technology meant you could be under observation every move you made, wherever you went.

He walked along Euston Road to the British Library. The whole time he still had the same uncomfortable feeling of being kept under watch. He made it to the big red-brick building, checked in his bag at the desk, and then went through to the reading rooms.

Lauren was sitting at one of the computer terminals, and she waved and smiled at him when she saw him walk in.

'Well?' she asked.

'It was a bust,' he admitted. 'I got there, and . . .'

A short but severe coughing sound of reprimand from the woman at the next computer terminal made him turn. The woman glared at him. Jake gave her an apologetic smile. He mimed drinking a cup of coffee, and Lauren nodded in agreement. She logged out of the computer, gathered up the sheets of paper she'd written her notes on, then she and Jake headed out of the reading room, for the coffee bar on the same floor.

After they'd sat down with their coffee, Jake told her glumly about his abortive trip to Muswell Hill.

'So, you can say, "I told you so," ' he said with a sigh.

'Not at all,' said Lauren. 'It *could* have been something. After all, The Index is out there somewhere.'

'But not in Muswell Hill,' groaned Jake. He gestured towards the reading room. 'How did you get on?'

'Brilliant!' Lauren smiled. 'They've got a copy of a really old herbal from the eleventh century, with recipes for cures for all sorts of diseases.'

Lauren was in the final year of a science degree, with her emphasis on Alternative Sciences.

'No Malichea book, then,' said Jake.

'No,' said Lauren. 'But not every ancient science text found its way into the Library of the Order.'

'Just the key ones,' said Jake.

'Mainly the ones threatened with destruction,' said Lauren. She sipped at her coffee and looked quizzically at Jake. 'You look worried,' she said. 'This Muswell Hill business?'

Jake shook his head.

'No. Like I said, that was either a practical joke, or – if it was serious – they'll get in touch later. No, I had this feeling I was being followed.'

'When?'

'On the way here. Right from the moment I got on the platform at Finsbury Park.'

Lauren frowned.

'Did you notice anyone in particular?'

Jake shook his head.

'No,' he said. He sighed. 'It could just be my imagination, but . . .'

He shrugged. Lauren looked around them, at the other people in the cafeteria, and those walking past, going about their business.

'No one looks particularly suspicious,' she whispered.

'They wouldn't if they were doing their job properly,' murmured Jake.

'Why would anyone be following you *now*?' Lauren frowned. 'Let's face it, it's been a while since we were actively involved in getting our hands on one of the hidden books.'

'Yes, but then there was this business of the phone call about The Index, and Muswell Hill.'

'A hoax,' said Lauren.

'Maybe,' admitted Jake.

They finished their coffee and went down to the check-in desk in the lower lobby to collect their bags. Lauren handed over her numbered plastic disc and collected hers. When the assistant returned with Jake's disc in his hand, he looked puzzled.

'I'm sorry,' he said. 'There seems to be some sort of confusion.'

'What sort of confusion?' asked Jake.

'The item of property related to this disc has gone. The disc is back in its place.'

Jake stared at the assistant, trying to get his brain around what was being said. He looked at the disc in the assistant's hand, the one he'd just handed over, a round plastic yellow disc with the number 19 in black. And then at a second disc the assistant produced: another yellow plastic disc, absolutely identical to the first, with that same number, 19, in black on it.

'But . . .' stammered Jake, bewildered. He looked again at the two identical plastic discs.

'You mean you have two discs here, with exactly the same number on them?' he asked, stunned.

The assistant shook his head.

'No, absolutely not,' he said. 'We only have one of each number. But it seems that this disc, number nineteen, has already been used to remove the item.'

'But it's my bag!' exploded Jake. 'Mine! I left it here! And I was given that disc!'

'I know that's what you say, sir, but we don't have duplicate discs . . .' began the assistant.

'Then who's taken my bag?' demanded Jake angrily.

The sound of Jake's raised voice, and the tone of

anger in it, brought a man in the uniform of a security guard hurrying over.

'Is there a problem?' he asked.

'Yes, there certainly is!' burst out Jake. 'Someone has stolen my bag!'

The assistant's face tightened and he said tersely, 'We don't know that for sure, sir. If you'd calm down . . . Are you sure you handed the bag into the counter in the first place?'

'Yes, and I was given that plastic disc!' snapped back Jake, exasperated. 'And if you ask the woman who gave me that disc, she'll confirm it was me. Ask your colleague to come here. A woman, about fifty, blonde hair. Glasses. Irish accent.'

'Dervla.' The assistant nodded. 'I'm afraid she's left for the day. Her shift's ended.'

'What about the person who handed in the disc and took the bag?' asked Lauren.

'They didn't give it to me,' said the assistant. 'The only other person who's been here this afternoon is Mo.' He turned and called, 'Mo!', and a young man in a uniform appeared from behind the scenes.

'Yes?' asked Mo.

The assistant held out the plastic disc with the number 19 on it.

'Did you take this in?' he asked.

Mo looked at the disc, then nodded.

'Yes,' he said. 'About five minutes ago.'

'Who collected it?' asked the security guard.

'A woman,' said Mo. 'In her early twenties, I'd guess.' He looked at Lauren. 'About your age and height. Black hair.'

'And she gave you this disc?' persisted Jake.

'Yes.' Mo nodded.

Jake turned to the security guard.

'You'd better call the police,' he said. 'Someone's stolen my bag.'

'We don't know that,' said the security guard defensively.

'Yes we do,' said Jake firmly. 'Check with this Dervla, she'll confirm, it was me who handed the bag in and the disc she gave me. And you've heard this man say he gave the bag to a woman.'

'I'm sure it must be just a mistake,' said the assistant in a hopeful tone. 'A mix-up.'

Jake pointed to the two identical yellow plastic discs, both with the number 19 on them.

'Not with those two, it's not,' he said.

The security guard looked at the two plastic discs, at Mo, and weighed up the situation. Then he announced, 'If you'd come with me to the office, we'll begin our investigation.'

Jake and Lauren followed the security guard to an inner office, where they discovered that 'beginning the investigation' meant filling in forms; in particular, Jake's name and address, a description of Jake's bag, and a list of the bag's contents. When that list consisted of a bar of chocolate, a bag of peanuts and a bottle of water, the security guard looked warily at Jake.

'Why would anyone want to steal these items?' he asked.

'I'm not saying they did,' said Jake. 'I'm saying they stole the bag, because of what they thought *might* be in it.'

'And what did they think might be in it?' asked the security guard.

'I don't know,' admitted Jake. 'Who knows how thieves think? They see a bag and snatch it, and then look to see what's in it.'

'But, if what you're saying is true, then there's a lot more to this than a casual bag-snatching,' pointed out the security guard. 'You're suggesting that someone prepared a duplicate disc, with the same number on it . . .'

'It needn't have been the same number already on it,' pointed out Jake. 'It could have been a blank disc, and when they saw the number I'd been given, they put that number, nineteen, on afterwards.'

'But why would they do that?' asked the security guard. 'Just for a small bag with some snacks in it? If it was a scam to steal a bag, surely they'd use that same blank disc and put a number on when they saw a bag that looked like it might contain something valuable.'

Because they didn't know what was in the bag, thought Jake. Whoever did this thought the bag held some information to do with the Order of Malichea, possibly about The Index. I was right, I was followed.

'I don't know,' said Jake. 'All I know is that someone used that duplicate disc to steal my bag from your cloakroom.'

'And we'll certainly report it to the police and investigate it,' said the security guard.

'I'll report it to the police as well,' said Jake. But in his heart he knew it was a waste of time. Whoever had snatched his bag had planned this carefully. Someone was after him. Again.

# Chapter 2

Jake and Lauren rode the Tube back to Finsbury Park in a kind of shock.

'The meeting at Muswell Hill wasn't a hoax,' said Jake. 'Someone else knew about it and thought I'd picked up some sort of information at that meeting, and they thought I'd put it in my bag for safe keeping.'

'But if they'd been watching you, they'd have known that the person didn't actually turn up. That you never actually met them,' pointed out Lauren.

'Maybe they couldn't be sure,' said Jake. 'They see people pass me by while I'm standing there, and for all they know someone had slipped something to me. A book. A piece of paper.'

Lauren shook her head.

'Who?' she asked.

'No idea,' admitted Jake. 'It could be any of the people we've come across since we started. Pierce

15

Randall. MI5. The Watchers. Or maybe it's somebody completely new.' He sighed. 'Anyway, for the moment we can forget about them. The only thing we know is they've got my bag.'

'Yes, but when they find out it's just got a bar of chocolate and a packet of nuts and a bottle of water, maybe they'll come after you again,' suggested Lauren.

'Good point,' muttered Jake. 'Once we get into the flat, we'll lock all the doors firmly and barricade ourselves in for the evening.'

'Do I get to choose which DVD we watch?' asked Lauren with a smile. 'Nothing too scary, I promise.'

Jake grinned.

'Sorry, I know I'm starting to get paranoid,' he said.

'It's only a bag,' stressed Lauren. 'We've been in a lot worse situations and come out of them OK.'

As they neared their small block of flats they were still joking about some of the life-threatening situations they'd been in, when suddenly Jake stopped in his tracks and any smile on his face vanished.

'What's the matter?' asked Lauren.

'Two men waiting outside our block,' he muttered.

Lauren followed his look, and gave a sharp intake of breath.

'I think we'd better go,' she murmured.

'Good idea,' said Jake.

He turned, and as he did so he found a large man standing in his way. A tall thin woman was beside the man. Both were holding out what appeared to be police warrant cards.

'Mr Jacob Wells? I'm Inspector Bullen from the CID. This is Detective Sergeant Aziz.'

Automatically, Jake stepped back, prepared to run, but out of the corner of his eye he saw the two men from his block of flats hurrying towards them. Inspector Bullen was still speaking, and as his words registered, Jake felt his mouth open in shock.

'I am arresting you on suspicion of being involved in the murder of Alexander Munro . . .'

'Munro!' Jake echoed. 'What?'

'You have the right to remain silent, but anything you say may be taken down and may be used as evidence,' continued Bullen. With that, he turned to the two men, who had now arrived. 'Handcuff Mr Wells and put him in the car.'

'No!' yelled Jake. 'I didn't do anything!'

As the two men took hold of Jake and handcuffed him, Lauren demanded, 'Where are you taking him? I'm his girlfriend and I'll be contacting his legal representative, so I insist on knowing where you are taking him.'

'We're not sure yet,' said Bullen. 'That depends.'

They're not real policemen, thought Jake with alarm. If they were, they'd name the station they're taking me to.

'Phone Gareth,' Jake said to Lauren. 'Tell him what's happened.'

'I need to know where you are taking him,' persisted Lauren doggedly.

'We're taking him to Holloway Road station,' said Bullen, 'but the chances are we'll be moving him on for questioning. If you give me your phone number, we'll contact you as soon as we know which station Mr Wells is being held at.'

'Phone Gareth!' repeated Jake urgently.

'Who is Gareth?' asked Bullen.

'You'll soon find out,' said Jake.

And let's hope I'm not exaggerating, thought Jake. Gareth Findlay-Weston, Jake's boss at the Department of Science and a covert section head of MI5, had pulled strings on Jake's behalf before. As the police officers pushed the handcuffed Jake into the back of the police car, Jake prayed that Gareth would be able to get him out of this one too.

The interview room was small, almost claustrophobic. The walls were painted a deep dark green, making it seem even smaller. There were no external windows; just one large internal blacked-out window in one wall.

People outside could see in, but people in the room couldn't see out. The overhead strip lights blazed harshly down.

Jake sat at the one table in the room looking at Detective Inspector Bullen, who sat opposite him. DS Usma Aziz sat next to DI Bullen. A uniformed constable stood by the door.

I should have someone here with me, thought Jake. This was the fourth or fifth time he'd found himself in a police interrogation room since he'd first become involved in the hidden library of the Order of Malichea. I should be used to it by now, he thought. But he wasn't. There was still that feeling of helplessness that came with being in a windowless room, with accusing glares from unsmiling police officers.

'Shouldn't I have a solicitor with me?' he asked.

'This is just an initial interview,' said Bullen.

'Yes, but I'm accused of murdering someone,' defended Jake.

'Do you have a solicitor?' asked Bullen. 'This person you mentioned? Gareth?'

No, thought Jake. I used to have Alex Munro at Pierce Randall, but now he's dead and I'm accused of killing him . . .

'No,' said Jake. 'But my partner, Lauren, will be arranging one through Gareth. He's my boss.'

'And Gareth's full name?' asked Bullen.

19

'Gareth Findlay-Weston at the Department of Science,' replied Jake. 'I'm a press officer there.'

He wondered whether DI Bullen knew that Gareth was a head of section with MI5. He doubted it. Gareth's true role as a spook was only known high up the chain of command.

He looked around the interrogation room. Jake had been relieved when they'd actually pulled up outside a police station. He'd been sure that they'd been fake police officers with fake IDs, the next stage of trying to find out what Jake had picked up from his meeting at Muswell Hill. But no, they'd brought him to a real police station.

'Has anyone told Lauren where I am?' asked Jake. 'She'll need to know in order to arrange my solicitor.'

'And I suppose she'll arrange it with this boss of yours,' said Bullen. 'Gareth.'

'Yes,' said Jake.

'He must be a very good boss if he doesn't mind being disturbed on a Saturday night,' said Bullen. 'We find that's very rare in the Civil Service.'

'Gareth is a very rare boss,' said Jake. 'And can you please answer my question: has anyone told Lauren where I am? You said you'd let her know.'

'That's all in hand,' said Bullen.

'I'm allowed a phone call,' said Jake. 'I'd like to make that call now. To Lauren. To tell her where I am.'

Bullen looked directly at Jake.

'If you give us her number, we'll make that call,' he said.

'She gave it to you already,' protested Jake. 'I saw her give it you. Anyway, I thought I was allowed to make the call myself.'

'That is a popular misconception.' Bullen nodded. 'And yes, she did give us her number. But just to make sure we're calling the right one, if you could give it to us yourself?'

Jake gritted his teeth to stop himself from shouting out loud angrily. He knew it wouldn't do him any good. He was sure they were playing for time, making sure they kept him for as long as possible without a lawyer being present; but there wasn't a lot he could do about it right now. They were in charge.

DI Bullen passed a piece of paper and a pen across the table to Jake, and Jake wrote Lauren's number down. Bullen took the pen back, and passed the piece of paper to DS Aziz.

'Tell her where Mr Wells is,' he said.

DS Aziz nodded, and got up and left the room, pulling the door shut after her.

'For the tape, DS Aziz has just left the room,' said Bullen. He turned back to Jake. 'As I said, this is just an initial interview to find out if there is a case against you.'

'So I haven't officially been arrested, as such?' asked Jake.

'You've been taken into custody because we had information that you may be able to help us with our enquiries,' said Bullen.

'What information?' asked Jake.

Bullen was silent for a moment, looking at Jake thoughtfully. Then he asked, 'Where were you at two o'clock this afternoon?'

'Why?' asked Jake. 'Was that when Munro was killed?'

Bullen seemed to soften his attitude a little.

'Look, Mr Wells, we can counter questions with questions all afternoon and just go round in circles, or — if you'd prefer — we can wait and see what happens about your solicitor. Although, with it being Saturday evening, my guess is that might take some time. Or, as I said, we can treat this as an initial interview to find out if there might be any substance to the suspicions concerning your involvement in the death of Mr Munro.'

'I had no involvement in it,' said Jake firmly. 'I haven't seen Alex Munro for months and months. I certainly didn't see him today.'

'But your name is in his dairy with an appointment for today. At 2 p.m.'

'I didn't have any appointment with Alex Munro, or with anyone else from Pierce Randall, today, or at any time recently.'

'Do you know a Guy de Courcey?' asked Bullen.

Jake shook his head.

'No,' he said. 'And I've never heard that name before, either.'

'According to Mr Munro's diary, he was due to meet you and Mr Guy de Courcey at the Red Hen Café in Crouch End Broadway at 2 p.m. this afternoon.'

Crouch End! The shock of it hit Jake. He was being set up! Framed!

Bullen gave Jake a questioning look, then said, 'You look as if that's triggered something, Mr Wells. Were you around the Red Hen Café in Crouch End Broadway this afternoon?'

'No,' said Jake. 'But I was driving past it.'

'And you didn't notice any disturbance in that area?'

I should wait until my lawyer gets here, thought Jake. But, as Bullen said, that could take ages. He didn't know if Lauren had even managed to get hold of Gareth. And, if she had, would Gareth want to get involved in this? Jake was sure he would once he knew it was Alex Munro who had been killed, but for all Jake knew, it had been Gareth who had had Munro killed.

'Mr Wells?' prompted Bullen.

'I'm being set up,' said Jake, reaching a decision. If he came clean with the police at this early stage, they might see he was innocent and let him go.

'Being set up?' repeated Bullen.

23

Jake nodded.

'I had a phone call telling me that if I went to Muswell Hill Broadway at half past one, I'd be contacted by someone who had some information that would help me.'

'What information was this?'

'About a book called The Index. It's an old book that was compiled by the Order of Malichea.'

The door opened and all eyes turned towards DS Aziz as she came back into the interview room.

'For the tape, DS Aziz returns to the interview,' said Bullen.

'I've told Ms Graham where you are,' Aziz said to Jake. 'She said she's arranging legal representation for you.'

'Did she say if she'd got hold of Gareth Findlay-Weston?' Jake asked.

'She didn't volunteer that information and I didn't ask her,' said Aziz.

'I should have made the call!' said Jake angrily.

'The phone call has been made and she's been notified,' said Bullen flatly. 'Now, can we return to the matter in hand. You were talking about something called the Order of Malichea.'

Jake glared at him. He wanted to pursue the business of his phone call, *demand* that he be allowed to speak to Lauren, but he knew arguing about it would just slow things down. He needed to get out of here as fast as he could.

'Yes.' Jake nodded.

'Are they a religious order?' asked Bullen.

'They were,' said Jake. 'They died out in 1539.'

'And this person you went to meet, they had a copy of this book?'

'I don't know,' said Jake. 'I doubt it. It's very rare, and people have been searching for it for years.'

'Why?' asked Bullen.

'Because of the information it contains.'

'What information?'

'It's said to be a list detailing where each of the books from the Library of Malichea were hidden,' said Jake. 'You see, the books in the library were forbidden.'

'Dirty books?' asked Bullen.

'No,' said Jake. 'Nothing like that. They were scientific texts, written over hundreds and hundreds of years. Right up until the library was hidden in 1497 by the monks. They hid the books because the sort of sciences described in them were considered heretical by the Church at the time, and if they were found . . .'

'Yes yes.' Bullen nodded impatiently. 'Can we get back to the present time. Today. So, you went to Muswell Hill?'

'Yes. I got there just before half past one and waited, but no one turned up. Then, at a quarter to two, I got a text from them saying they couldn't make it after all. So I drove back home.'

'Through Crouch End Broadway?'

'Yes,' said Jake. 'That's the most direct route to Finsbury Park from Muswell Hill.'

'So you would have been in Crouch End Broadway at about 2 p.m.?'

'No. I was driving *through* Crouch End Broadway about ten minutes or so before two o'clock. As I've told you already, I left Muswell Hill at a quarter to two. The road was pretty clear.'

'We've checked with the CCTV cameras in the area, and they show your car in the area of Crouch End Broadway at 1.54 p.m.'

'OK. So it was six minutes to two.'

'But you were in the area. You could have parked . . .'

'But I didn't! Look, check my mobile phone records. You'll find the text I told you I got telling me the person couldn't make it, and the time. Quarter to two.'

Bullen nodded.

'We will,' he said.

'And I never had a meeting of any sort scheduled with Alex Munro,' Jake repeated firmly. 'So, like I say, if my name's in his diary for this afternoon, then it's obvious that someone's framing me. Especially when you add in the mystery person who fixed up the meeting in Muswell Hill, and then cancelled, knowing full well I'd be getting to Crouch End right at the time Munro was being killed. It's a set-up!'

'Who would want to frame you for Mr Munro's murder?' asked Bullen.

Loads of people, thought Jake. Nearly everyone I've ever met who've been involved in the Malichea business.

'I don't know,' admitted Jake. 'But it wouldn't surprise me to find out it's the same people who stole my bag today.'

Bullen frowned.

'Stole your bag?' he repeated.

'Yes.' Jake nodded. 'From the British Library. You can check. Their security people said they'd be reporting it to the police, and I said I'd be reporting it too. So, you can start taking details of that, as well.'

'We will. But first, I'd like to concentrate on what happened at Crouch End Broadway.'

'I've told you, I had nothing to do with that!'

'And this Guy de Courcey . . .'

'I've already told you, I don't know anyone called Guy de Courcey!' snapped Jake angrily. 'Look, I've tried to tell you that I've been framed, and that this could be linked to my bag being stolen from the British Library today. Someone who the staff at the British Library can describe to you. But you don't seem interested! We've had our initial chat, as you call it, and I've told you the truth. I'm not saying anything more until I've seen my solicitor.'

Bullen hesitated, then nodded.

'Very well,' he said. 'We'll get on to the British Library and see what they say. And, as soon as your solicitor gets in touch, we'll talk again. Until then, the constable will take you to a cell.'

'But I'm innocent!' protested Jake. 'I've told you what happened!'

'We need to check out some of what you've said. Until then, we'll need to keep you here for when your solicitor arrives.' For the tape, he added, 'Interview terminated at 7.30 p.m.' Then he gestured to the uniformed constable by the door. 'Constable, take Mr Wells to cell number two.'

# Chapter 3

Lauren dialled the number again. So far she'd tried Gareth's home number six times, and on each occasion all she'd got was an answerphone with a mechanical voice asking her to leave a message. This time she got a real voice.

'Hello?' said a woman.

Lauren was aware of the nervous tone in her voice. But then, that could be because her husband was involved in the espionage business, and you'd always be worried about who might be calling.

'Can I speak to Mr Gareth Findlay-Weston, please?' she asked. 'It's urgent.'

'I'm afraid Mr Findlay-Weston isn't here,' said the woman.

'When will he be back?' asked Lauren.

'I'm sorry, I can't help you,' said the woman. 'Goodbye.'

'No!' shouted Lauren. 'Please! My name's Lauren Graham. Mr Findlay-Weston knows me. Jake Wells needs his help. He's been arrested on a false charge of killing Alex Munro . . .'

'I'm sorry, I can't help you,' repeated the woman. 'Goodbye.'

And this time the phone was hung up.

'I'm not letting it go like that,' said Lauren grimly to herself; and she redialled the number. This time she got the recorded answerphone announcement, the mechanical voice asking her to leave a message.

Damn!

The turnkey unlocked the cell and gestured Jake inside. As the heavy metal door clanged shut behind him, Jake saw that there was someone else already in the cell, a young man in his early twenties. He was sitting on a bench, and he looked up inquisitively at Jake.

'Let me guess,' said the young man. 'You must be Jacob Wells.'

The young man's accent was right out of the upper class; a clipped drawl.

'Yes,' said Jake warily. 'Who are you?'

'I'm Guy de Courcey. I believe you're my alleged fellow-conspirator.'

'I had nothing to do with any murder!' snapped Jake.

'You and me both.' Guy nodded. 'But it's worth saying it for the tape.'

'What tape?' queried Jake, looking around.

'A hidden mic somewhere,' said Guy. 'It's the only reason I can think of for the police putting us together, hoping we'll say something that will incriminate us. Unless there's a shortage of cells in this place, of course. Which is possible. After all, it's a Saturday night. Great night for street brawls.' He grinned. 'So, do you prefer Jacob or Jake?'

'Jake,' said Jake despite himself. There was a lot about the young man's superior attitude that annoyed him, but at the same time he couldn't help but admit that he also had some charm. It was in his smile and his confident manner. Despite being locked up in a police cell, Guy de Courcey didn't seem at all troubled by the situation. The opposite in fact: he appeared almost amused about the whole thing.

'Have the police told you that we apparently had a meeting with this Alex Munro this afternoon?' Guy asked.

'Yes.' Jake sat down on the other bench in the cell. It was hard, just a concrete shelf. 'I told them I didn't have any such meeting. Not today, or any other day.'

'I did,' said Guy. 'But not in a café in Crouch End at two o'clock. My appointment with him was for ten tomorrow morning at his office. I was nowhere near Crouch End at two o'clock.'

'So, you've got an alibi?'

'Yes, but it's certainly not one the police are taking seriously. I was asleep in a hotel room the whole afternoon. And alone. Jet lag. That doesn't count as an alibi as far they are concerned.' He regarded Jake with an intrigued frown. 'Are you saying that you don't even know this Munro character?'

'No,' said Jake, shaking his head. 'I've met him, but not for a long time. I certainly haven't had any contact with him for months.'

'Yet the police say your name was in his diary, along with mine.'

Jake shrugged.

'Someone's setting me up,' he said.

'The police?' asked Guy. He shook his head. 'From my experience, the police in this country don't set you up as blatantly as they do in some others.' He looked at Jake in a superior way, and added, 'Well, they might set people like *you* up. But generally, they play honest where I'm concerned.' He gave a smile. 'That's one of the advantages of having a title.'

Jake frowned.

'A title?' he echoed.

'Viscount Guy de Courcey. At least, I was, but now I guess I'm the new earl, since the old man died.' He

32

gave Jake a broad grin. 'Yes, you are sharing a prison cell with the Earl de Courcey.'

'Am I supposed to be impressed?' Jake asked sarcastically.

Guy shrugged.

'No,' he said. 'But a lot of people are. It's amazing what having a title does. You can get tables in exclusive restaurants, seats for concerts . . .'

'And put in a police cell,' pointed out Jake.

Guy laughed and Jake's animosity towards the young earl faded slightly. Anyone who could laugh at himself couldn't be all bad.

'Good point,' chuckled Guy. 'Though with me, it's an occupational hazard, one I've become used to. Which is why I guess that right now, some poor bored copper is sitting listening to our words of wisdom through a hidden microphone somewhere in this cell.' He gestured towards the light fitting, which was set high in the ceiling and protected by a wire cage. 'Possibly there. Maybe even a closed-circuit TV camera to keep an eye on us. That's how they do it in some of the places I've been.'

'You sound like you've been in this situation a few times,' said Jake, intrigued in spite of himself.

'Usually only overnight stays, or for a few days, in places like Honduras, Brazil, Mexico. Like I say, once they discover I'm from a titled family, they see dollar signs, and up until recently the family solicitor has generally bailed me out.'

'I would have thought your family solicitor would have been here already, bailing you out of this one,' said Jake.

Guy shook his head.

'I decided against contacting him. He doesn't like me, thinks I'm a wastrel. And he's very old-fashioned. You can tell that from his name: Montague Ainsworth of Hapgood, Ainsworth and Ainsworth. This new chap, Alex Munro from Randall Pierce, he sounded interesting. The sort who'd be prepared to cut a few corners. Bend the rules.'

'Oh yes, he most definitely is,' said Jake. Then he corrected himself. 'Was,' he added. 'How did you meet Munro?'

'I never actually met him,' admitted Guy. 'He tracked me down to a little place in Mexico, my last port of call. He phoned me up and offered me a plane ticket back to England and all my expenses paid, as well as taking care of some debts. And I have a few of those.'

'Why would he do that?'

'He wanted to talk to me about some outfit called the Order of Malichea.'

Jake guessed that would be at the heart of this. The murder of Alex Munro. Himself being framed and

34

arrested. But where did his aristocratic cellmate fit in? Or was he a new player in the game?

'Why you?' asked Jake.

'Because it seems my family had some of their books.'

Jake felt a surge of excitement that he tried hard not to show.

'Which books?'

'According to Munro, one of them was the *Journal of the Order*,' said Guy. 'You know, the diary of the Order. What went on from year to year. Boring stuff. "Got up. Prayed. Civil War again." That sort of thing. The other was something called The Index.'

The Index! thought Jake, and now he found it even harder not to show his excitement. Surely this was why Munro had been murdered.

'Anyway, Pierce Randall seemed the right kind of lawyers to have on your side,' continued Guy. 'So I phoned them when I was arrested. I expected them to be here by now.' Then he sighed and added, 'Though they could be having second thoughts, seeing as I'm charged with killing their boss.'

'So, you must know quite a bit about the Order of Malichea,' said Jake, trying to appear casual.

Guy shook his head.

'Nothing. I was hoping this character, Munro, would tell me all about them, and these books he was all het up about. But then, the de Courceys have never been that hot on things like books — more hunting, shooting, fishing and gambling. Although there have been a few Churchy types in the family, way back. Not that I know much about them. The old man was always telling me I ought to find out about our family history and the family home, but whatever he told me to do only made sure I didn't do it.'

'So where is the family home?' asked Jake.

'De Courcey Hall in Kent. At least, it *was* the family home. It isn't any more.' He gave a sigh. 'Sold, along with everything else.' He chuckled and added, 'As a family, we've been broke for hundreds of years, ever since we backed the wrong side in the Civil War. The de Courceys backed Charles I. What they should have done is what all the rest of the aristocracy did: back both sides. Anyway, since then things went downhill, money-wise. And every time another earl died, it piled up more and more death duties. That's why my father decided to get rid of the hall and everything in it.

'He tried to sell it, but no one wanted it. I'm not surprised, the place is huge and damp. It would cost the budget of a small country just to heat it. So, in the end, he gave it to the National Trust, just before he died. The small amount of money left over from the sale of the contents went into a family trust to tide me over until I reach the age of twenty-five. Then, if there's anything left, it goes to charity.'

'Charity? You mean you get nothing?'

Guy shrugged.

'Fair's fair,' he said. 'The old man guessed that if he left it to me I'd just drink it away. So, I'm doing my best to spend what I can of it in the next three years. I've overspent most of it already.'

'But the library? Did that go to the National Trust as well?'

'Most of it, though I think the old man kept some of the books. The rarest ones.' Guy looked at Jake with his air of studied world-weariness, and asked, 'Do you know anything about this Order of Malichea?'

'Quite a lot,' said Jake.

'Well, maybe you can fill me in,' said Guy. 'After all, it's Saturday night, and there's no sign yet of our solicitors. It'll be as good a way to pass the time as any.'

Yes, thought Jake. Though the young earl was a self-confessed rogue — unless he'd been exaggerating — there might be some memory of the ancient books from his childhood at de Courcey Hall, and maybe telling him about the Order and the hidden books might trigger something. It might even lead Jake to The Index.

'OK,' said Jake. 'The story starts way back in the seventh century, on the island of Lindisfarne.'

'Oh my God,' groaned Guy. 'That far back? This is going to take for ever!'

'Not that long,' Jake reassured him.

'OK,' said Guy. 'So, what happened on Lindisfarne in . . . whenever?'

'A monk founded a monastery there. Over the years, as word about it spread, scholars from across the world came to exchange scientific research. Then the Spanish Inquisition came. Because lots of the scientific works in their library were by Arabic or Islamic scholars, and quite a few dated from pre-Christian Roman or Greek times, most of them would be considered heretical, as would any texts that went against the orthodox Church view of the world.'

'So they'd be destroyed,' commented Guy.

'Absolutely,' said Jake. 'To save the texts from destruction, they moved the library to Glastonbury Abbey, where they hid the books in secret rooms behind the official library. But the threat spread, and the leader of the Order of Malichea instructed the monks of the Order to take these so-called "heretical" science books and hide them in a place that was unlikely to be disturbed because it was either sacred, or said to be cursed, or claimed to be haunted. A coded list of the different books and their hiding places was kept, known as The Index. The intention was for the books to stay hidden until the threat of the Inquisition had passed, and then the books could be recovered.'

'So what happened?'

'The plague. It returned to Britain and wiped out a huge percentage of the population, including many of the monks who had hidden the scientific texts. With them went the knowledge of where they'd hidden them. The only evidence that these "lost sciences" actually existed and had been hidden was in the *Journal of the Order of Malichea*, which was a history of the Order handed down through the ages, and The Index, the list of where the scientific books were hidden.'

'Bummer,' murmured Guy. 'So where do we come in? The de Courceys?'

'I'm not sure,' admitted Jake. 'Your family could have been tied in with the Order? Or, maybe, with Henry VIII.'

'Yes, now that is quite likely.' Guy nodded. 'There are paintings in the hall, or, rather, there used to be, with the earl at the time and Henry VIII.' He looked inquisitively at Jake. 'But why would my family being pally with King Henry tie us in with these missing books?'

'The Dissolution of the Monasteries,' explained Jake. 'Henry VIII ordered most of the monasteries to be shut down. It was part of his getting rid of the old Catholic religion and replacing it with one of his own, the Church of England.

'Henry VIII's forces looted the abbey at Glastonbury and the books in the priory's library came into the hands of the king, and so into the possession of the State. But it's not known what happened to The Index or the *Journal of the Order of Malichea*.'

'According to Munro, he thinks they ended up in our family library,' said Guy. 'Are they worth much? I expect so, if Munro was prepared to pay for me to come all the way back here from Mexico.'

'Millions,' said Jake. 'Possibly billions.'

Guy stared at Jake, and for the first time his air of casual nonchalance had vanished. He looked at Jake, his mouth open in bewilderment.

'Billions?' he echoed.

'Billions.' Jake nodded.

'But . . . just for a couple of old books? Why?'

'Not so much the *Journal of the Order of Malichea*, it's The Index that's the valuable one. Because it's said to show where every one of the books was hidden.'

'But . . . but so what? These are just old books!'

'No,' Jake corrected him. 'These are books that are said to contain some secrets of science that had to remain hidden because they were seen as heretical. Books about time travel, invisibility . . .'

'Sci-fi and fantasy,' chuckled Guy.

'Not all of them,' said Jake. 'I saw the effects of the science of one of them when a book was dug up and opened accidentally. It was about creating food from the water in the air. A sort of fungus. The trouble was, the fungus grew all over the poor bloke who found it.'

'Did it kill him?' asked Guy.

'I'm not sure,' said Jake.

'That would make a powerful weapon,' said Guy thoughtfully. 'I can see people paying for that.'

'And for some of the other stuff. There are said to be cures for cancer, and other serious illnesses. Can you imagine how much the patents on those would be worth to a drug company!'

Guy nodded, and Jake could almost see the young earl's mind calculating his new wealth.

'And I own it,' he murmured, awed.

Jake shook his head.

'Whoever's got the books owns them. And whoever has The Index . . .'

'Knows where the books are hidden,' finished Guy.

'Exactly,' said Jake.

Guy smiled and stretched back on the bench.

'Jake, my friend, I think this unfortunate death of Mr Munro, leading to us being thrown in this cell together, could be the beginning of a whole new and very profitable partnership. Your knowledge of this business, and mine about our family and the library.'

'I'm not in the hunt for the books for profit,' said Jake.

'Oh, I'm sure we can come to some arrangement,' said Guy. 'Now, it could be jet lag, but my body thinks it's about time I had some sleep.' He looked at Jake and smiled again. 'Wake me up if my solicitor arrives, will you.'

# Chapter 4

Jake lay on the bunk in the cell, listening to Guy snoring. Without his watch or his mobile, he had no idea what the time was. There were no windows to the outside. The light behind the protective wire mesh in the ceiling had been turned down, but not switched off. The fact it had been turned down, so it didn't glow so brightly, told Jake that it was night-time. But whether it was midnight, or two in the morning, he could only guess.

Jake's thoughts turned to Alex Munro. Dead. Shot through the head, according to the police. He remembered his first meeting with Munro, when the solicitor had promised Jake everything — as much money as he wanted and Lauren's freedom — if he would work with him and his law firm, Pierce Randall, to find the missing Malichea books.

Munro had been lying, of course. Munro always lied and schemed and double-crossed.

Was that what had happened? That Munro had double-crossed the wrong person? Because most of Pierce Randall's clients were very dangerous people: as well as governments, they represented international gangsters, terrorists, dubious dictators. Any of those people wouldn't think twice about having someone killed. But why Munro?

One thing was certain: whoever had done it had gone to some lengths to frame Jake for the murder. Which meant whoever it was knew about Jake and his interest in the books. So his instinct had been right: he had been under surveillance.

Jake's thoughts flitted to the Watchers, the mysterious organisation set up way back in the fifteenth century to keep watch over the hidden books and protect them from being discovered. At first the Watchers had been cooks, servants, carpenters, stonemasons. Trusted tradespeople who'd worked at the abbey in Glastonbury. As time passed, the role of Watcher had been handed down from generation to generation. Parents to their children. Uncles and aunts to nieces and nephews. They were still ordinary people doing ordinary jobs — nurses, teachers, railway workers, taxi drivers, carpenters, journalists.

But peaceful, Jake murmured to himself. The Watchers' creed was no violence, but to protect the books at all costs.

Of course, there had been renegades. Perhaps one with the skill and commitment to blow someone's head off and frame someone else for it.

So many questions nagged at Jake. Why frame him now? Why kill Alex Munro? Where was Lauren? And where was Gareth, and why hadn't he got Jake out of here!

Jake woke. There was a humming noise.

For a moment he was disorientated, couldn't work out where he was. He was lying on something hard. And then, as he opened his eyes and saw the walls of the cell and smelt the disinfectant, he remembered.

He sat up, and saw Guy sitting on his bunk, smiling at him. It was Guy who'd been humming a tune.

'Welcome back to the land of the living,' said Guy.

'I'd hoped it had all been a dreadful dream,' groaned Jake.

'Afraid not,' said Guy. 'We're still locked up.' He sighed. 'I wish I knew what time it was. My stomach tells me it's breakfast, but I could still be working on Mexican time. Or it could be just that I haven't eaten in ages. Aren't they supposed to feed us? That's one thing about the prisons in Latin America, you get fed. Mainly beans, but at least it's food. I'm sure withholding food from us is a breach of our human rights, or something.'

The sound of a key jangling in the lock made them both turn towards the door.

'Looks like breakfast after all!' Guy grinned.

The door opened and a police constable looked in. There was no sign of a tray, or any smell of food.

'OK, you two,' he said. 'Your briefs are here. You can go. Pick up your things at reception.'

Jake's brain was not quite taking this in. What had changed? Had Gareth swung into action?

'Yess!' exulted Guy. 'Freedom, here we come!'

He headed for the door. Jake hurried after him, worried that the door might slam shut before he got out.

Jake and Guy followed the uniformed constable along the corridor, then up the stairs to the main police station. The first person he saw was Lauren, who rushed towards him and threw her arms around him.

'How are you?' she asked. 'Did they treat you all right?'

'Apart from keeping me locked up, and not knowing what was going on,' grumbled Jake.

He looked towards where a man in a dark suit was in discussion with the desk sergeant and filling in forms.

'So, Gareth came through,' said Jake.

Lauren shook her head.

'I couldn't get hold of him,' she said.

'Then who's the guy in the suit?'

'He's from Pierce Randall. He's representing the other man they're holding.'

'Guy de Courcey,' said Jake. 'So, where's *my* solicitor?'

'Bex!' called Lauren.

Jake was suddenly aware of a young woman in her early twenties, dressed in extreme goth fashion, who was engaged in a deep conversation with a uniformed constable. The young woman, Bex, turned, and came towards Jake and Lauren.

'Bex was at uni with me,' explained Lauren. 'She was studying Law. She's just graduated.' Almost apologetically, she added to Jake in a whisper, 'She was the only person I could get at short notice on a Saturday night.'

'Hi!' Bex beamed. 'You must be Jake.'

'Yes.' Jake smiled. 'Thanks for getting me out.' Then, frowning, he asked Bex, 'I assume I am being released?'

'Absolutely.' Bex nodded. 'The Force is with us!' Then she added, 'Mind, it's only on a temporary basis.'

'How temporary?'

'You know, bail conditions. And you've got to hand in your passport. I told them you'd bring it in later today. Which obviously means you can't leave the country.'

'Bail?' asked Jake. 'How much bail? And who puts it up?'

Bex shook her head.

'This is police bail, under the Police and Criminal Evidence Act 1984,' she said. 'It relates back to Sections 3, 3A, 5 and 5A of the Bail Act 1976, where a suspect is released without being charged.'

Jake shot Lauren a quick glance to show he was impressed.

Bex continued, 'Basically, it means you're out, but they can call you back for further questioning.'

'Being out is good,' said Jake.

'Anyway,' said Bex, 'I've filled in most of the forms. All you have to do is sign them.'

'Thanks,' said Jake, with more enthusiasm this time.

'OK.' Bex smiled. She turned to Lauren. 'Thanks for this, Laur. It was great! I mean, this is a *murder* case! How cool is that!' She smiled again, said, 'Ciao!', and then headed for the door.

Jake looked after Bex as she disappeared, still bewildered by what had happened.

'You sure she's really a goth?' he asked.

Lauren shook her head.

'This week,' she said. 'Last week she was a preppy. She tries different phases. I think she's checking out which one works for her.'

'All that stuff about section this and section that was impressive,' said Jake admiringly.

'You want my opinion, being a lawyer works for her.'

'Jake!'

Jake turned and saw Guy standing beside them, still smiling, although Jake was sure there was more than a hint of relief in Guy's smile this time, for all his bravado about being used to being locked up in various prisons.

'Guy,' said Jake, 'this is Lauren, my girlfriend.'

'A pleasure.' Guy beamed. 'I'm Guy de Courcey.'

He held out his hand and Lauren shook it.

'*Earl* Guy de Courcey,' said Jake. 'He's an aristocrat.'

'But a very poor one.' Guy grinned. Turning back to Jake, he said, 'Actually, I was wondering if you felt like getting together later today, after I've got myself cleaned up. It appears I'm involved in the business of these books, whether I like it or not, and you seem to know all about them, so I'd like to pick your brains some more.'

'Lauren knows a lot more about them than I do,' said Jake.

'Then perhaps you'd both like to join me for a spot of lunch.' He jerked his thumb at the man in the dark suit, who was still talking to the desk sergeant. 'My new solicitors appear happy to pay my bill for the moment, so we might as well take advantage of it.'

49

'Actually, Pierce Randall also know a great deal about the hidden library of Malichea,' said Lauren.

'Yes, but they'll only tell me what they want me to know,' said Guy, dropping his voice to a whisper. 'Whereas you two, you've been there, from what Jake tells me. So, how about it? Lunch on me?'

'Great!' Jake nodded. 'Twelve o'clock?'

'Twelve it is. The Belvedere in the Strand. Just ask for me. I'll reserve us a table in the restaurant.'

'That's everything ready, Lord de Courcey,' said a voice.

They turned to see the solicitor from Pierce Randall standing beside them.

He looked tough. Slimly built and tall, with piercing eyes, up close Jake could see that his clothes were the best. As always, with everyone involved with Pierce Randall, money spoke.

'Excellent!' Guy smiled.

'I have a car waiting outside for you,' added the solicitor.

'Good.' Turning back to Jake and Lauren, Guy asked, 'In case I need to get in touch with you, let me have your phone number.'

'Sure,' said Jake. 'When I pick up my mobile and my other stuff from the desk sergeant, I'll phone mine through to you. What's your number?'

'Small problem,' sighed Guy. 'I haven't got myself sorted out with a UK mobile yet.' Gesturing towards the solicitor, he said, 'These guys are going to do that for me. But I can always use the hotel phone till then.'

'OK,' said Jake hesitantly. He wrote his mobile number down on a piece of paper, and gave it to Guy.

'Great!' said Guy. 'See you two later.'

With that, he followed his solicitor out of the police station.

Jake went over to the desk.

'So, is that everything for me too?' he asked. 'Can I take my things and go?'

'Not quite,' said the desk sergeant. 'There are some forms to sign, and you have to make an appointment to bring in your passport.'

'Fine,' said Jake. 'Let's have the forms.'

The young man watched from across the street as Jake Wells and Lauren Graham got into their car.

The sniper rifle he'd used to kill Alex Munro was safe, destroyed. There was no chance of that ever being used as evidence leading to him.

The next stage in his plan was Jake Wells and his girlfriend.

It was all about The Index. The Holy Grail. That one book with an untold worth. And it was going to be his. But to get his hands on it he had to be careful, and clever. Put the right amount of pressure on the right people. Tighten the screws. Cause some pain.

As he watched Jake and Lauren drive off, he smiled to himself.

Wait till you get back to your flat, he thought. You're in for a big surprise. A very unpleasant surprise.

# Chapter 5

As Lauren drove them back to their flat, Jake filled her in on Guy de Courcey.

'If Pierce Randall are to be believed, his family had The Index and the *Journal of the Order of Malichea* in their library at their stately home until very recently.'

'You're joking!' exclaimed Lauren. 'The Index!'

'That's what Guy said Alex Munro told him.'

'And then someone shot Alex Munro and framed you for it.'

'Me and Guy,' said Jake.

'Why?' asked Lauren.

Jake shrugged.

'Who knows? To divert attention away from the real murderer and get away with it, I suppose.'

'Yes, but why you, particularly? And why this Guy character?'

'I've no idea,' said Jake. He frowned. 'Tell me again about Gareth. About not being able to get hold of him.'

'That's all there is to tell,' said Lauren. 'I phoned his house, and I spoke to his wife, who hung up on me. At least, I assume it was his wife. I'll tell you one thing, she sounded really frightened.'

'I'm still a bit puzzled as to why the police let me go so easily,' said Jake. 'Even with your friend Bex and all that stuff about bail regulations.'

'Maybe they didn't,' said Lauren.

'They had enough to hold me,' pointed out Jake. 'The entry in Munro's diary. The CCTV footage of me in our car in Crouch End at the right time. But they let me go. And without a high-powered solicitor, or Gareth, to threaten them on my behalf.'

'I was surprised that Bex seemed to get you released so quickly,' admitted Lauren. 'I mean, Bex knows quite a bit about the law, but she's not the sort of lawyer who's going to scare the police. Maybe they felt that if they were letting Guy de Courcey go, they had to let you go as well.'

'It doesn't work that way, though, does it.' Jake shook his head. 'I think there's more going on here than the police said.'

'Gareth pulling the strings behind the scenes?'

'Maybe. Or someone else is.'

They reached their block of flats, and Lauren parked. They caught the lift up, and unlocked the door of their flat. Jake was about to walk in, but Lauren stopped him and peered round the partly open door. Then she told him, 'Someone's been in here.'

'What?!' said Jake. 'How can you tell?'

'After what happened with your bag being taken from the British Library, and then you being arrested, I got a bit scared. Say there really is someone after you. Or after whatever they think you had in that case. So I left a small box just behind the door. If anyone opened the door, the box would be pushed back. But the intruder wouldn't notice it, because the box was light.' She stepped in and pointed at a small cardboard box behind the door. 'There,' she said. 'It's moved back from where I left it.'

'Wow,' said Jake admiringly. 'You are so cool! You could be a secret agent.'

'Be serious!' said Lauren impatiently. 'Someone's been in our flat!' A sudden alarming thought struck her, and she whispered, 'Maybe they're still here!'

Jake shook his head.

'No,' he said. 'These people are professionals. You can tell by the fact that the lock and the door haven't been damaged. Professionals like that would have someone outside watching for us to come home, and they'd alert whoever was in here and get them out.'

'Unless they're deliberately waiting for us in there,' whispered Lauren.

'Good point,' admitted Jake. 'OK, you go and stand outside. Dial 999 on your mobile and keep your thumb ready poised to press "call" if I yell out.'

'Say they don't give you a chance to yell out?' asked Lauren. 'Do you think we ought to call the police?'

'And tell them what?'

'That we think someone's in our flat.'

Jake weighed it up. It made sense. If there really *was* someone in their flat, waiting for them, it would be foolish to just walk in.

But, if someone was after them, surely they'd have snatched them before they actually got into the flat. Unless they didn't want to risk attracting witnesses. Inside their flat, there'd be no one to see.

'Well?' demanded Lauren.

'I'll take a chance,' said Jake.

He stepped inside. This is crazy, he admitted to himself. If there is anyone in here, all they have to do is wait until I step into the room where they're hiding, and knock me out, or tazer me, or whatever they plan to do. And do it before I can shout out to Lauren to warn her.

'I'm going to keep talking all the time!' Jake called to Lauren. 'If I stop talking, run and call the police.'

With that he moved slowly along the short hallway. He could feel his heart beating faster. Calm, he told himself. Keep calm.

'The kitchen first,' he called. The door was open, and he could see at a glance there was no one in the tiny kitchen.

'Kitchen clear!' he called. 'Moving on to the bathroom next.'

The bathroom door was shut.

'OK, I'm at the bathroom door,' he announced. He wondered if Lauren could hear the fear in his voice.

Keep it cool, he told himself urgently.

He pushed the door handle down, and then shoved the door open hard, at the same time leaping to one side in case anyone had a gun aimed at the doorway.

There was no movement or sound at all from the bathroom.

He was sweating now, trying to hold himself together, expecting at any moment someone to appear, armed with a gun or a knife.

'Going into the bathroom!' he called. 'And counting, one, two, three . . .'

There was no one in the bathroom. He let out a sigh of relief.

'Bathroom clear!' he called.

He moved on to the bedroom. The door was closed.

'OK, I'm about to go into the bedroom!' he said. 'I'll keep counting!'

He opened the door and stepped carefully in, all the time counting out loud so that Lauren could hear him, 'One, two, three, four, five . . .'

No one was in the room. He went to the wardrobe, still counting out loud the whole time, pulled the door open and stepped back sharply, just in case anyone was hiding inside.

'Bedroom's clear!' he called. 'I'm moving on to the living room!'

Still counting out loud the whole time so that Lauren could hear, still petrified and waiting to be attacked, he edged carefully into the living room. Everything looked the same, undisturbed.

'There's no one here . . .' he began, and then he stopped.

'What the hell's that?!' demanded Lauren, shocked, and he saw she'd come in and, like him, was staring at the window.

There, in large letters on the glass, someone had written 'Malichea'. Underneath was added: 'Next time you die'.

Jake could feel his heart pounding harder than ever and his throat had gone dry.

'I'm calling the police,' said Lauren. 'When they see this it will prove there's someone after us!'

Jake shook his head.

'They might think that we wrote it ourselves. It's obvious that DI Bullen is suspicious of me.'

Lauren sank down on to the settee. She looked as shaken as Jake felt.

'I can't live like this,' she complained.

'It's the price we pay for getting mixed up with the hidden library.'

'But we haven't been involved for ages!' Lauren pointed out.

'Someone thinks we are,' said Jake. He pointed at the words on the glass. 'And now, with this, and me under suspicion of killing Alex Munro, it looks like we're well and truly involved again.'

'So, what's our way out of it?' asked Lauren.

'I think our only way out is going to be working with fellow-accused, Guy de Courcey,' said Jake. 'If Pierce Randall can get him off, then maybe the case against me will collapse as well.'

'And maybe, working with him, we might even get our hands on The Index,' said Lauren.

'Which is a long shot,' pointed out Jake. 'But, if we can, then that will solve everything.'

# Chapter 6

They entered the palatial reception area of the Belvedere Hotel as the ornate clock behind the desk was striking twelve. Not loud bongs, but discreet musical chimes fitting to the aura of elegance of a time gone by. There was a distinct air of money here: old money, new money, any money, so long as there was a lot of it. Guy de Courcey claimed he was broke, and his family had always been hard up, but Jake was sure that a hotel like this would have still been the kind of place where they would have stayed when in London.

The furniture, the decor, even the uniforms that the hotel staff wore all looked as if they were from the London of Charles Dickens. As Pierce Randall were picking up the bill, it was definitely the right place for the recently ennobled Earl Guy de Courcey.

Jake and Lauren approached the desk, where the receptionist on duty smiled a greeting at them.

'May I help you?' he enquired politely.

'Yes,' said Jake. 'We're here to meet Guy de Courcey. Could you ring his room and let him know we're here. Jake Wells and Lauren Graham.'

The receptionist gave them an apologetic look.

'I'm afraid Lord de Courcey checked out,' he said.

Jake and Lauren exchanged bewildered looks.

'Checked out?' repeated Jake. 'When?'

'This morning.'

'But . . . we only saw him a couple of hours ago,' said Jake, bewildered. 'And we arranged to see him here at twelve o'clock. Did he leave any message for us?'

The receptionist shook his head.

'I'm afraid not, sir. He left no messages.'

'He didn't say *anything* when he left about people calling to see him?'

The receptionist hesitated, then said, 'Actually, Lord de Courcey did not check out himself. He sent an emissary, who paid his bill and collected his belongings.'

'Did this emissary have a name?' asked Lauren.

'I'm sorry, I can't give out that kind of information,' said the receptionist.

'What did this emissary look like?' asked Jake desperately.

The receptionist looked suspiciously at Jake and Lauren.

'Are you asking these questions in any kind of official capacity?' he asked. 'If so, I would appreciate it if you

61

could show me some documentation, because we make it a practise never to discuss our clients.'

Wary of journalists looking for gossip, thought Jake. He shook his head.

'No,' he said. 'It's just that we're concerned for his safety and we wanted to make sure that nothing unfortunate had happened to him.'

The receptionist studied them both silently for a while, then said politely but firmly, 'I'm afraid I have nothing more to add. Now, if you'll excuse me . . .' With that, he turned away from them and went to attend to a couple who had just arrived at the desk.

Jake and Lauren headed across the reception area towards the door.

'What do you think?' asked Lauren.

'Pierce Randall,' said Jake grimly. 'That solicitor overheard Guy arranging to meet us, and was determined to stop that happening. They know what we think of them. They wouldn't want us interfering in their plans for The Index. If you ask me, once they'd got him in that car they had waiting, they whisked him away somewhere we can't get to him.'

'That's possible.'

Just then, Jake's phone rang. He checked it.

'A text,' he said.

He opened the text. There was one short message of three letters: 'hlp'.

Jake frowned and showed it to Lauren.

'What do you make of that?' he asked.

'Help,' said Lauren.

'Who's asking for help?' asked Jake.

He checked the number. It was withheld.

'Guy,' he said grimly.

'How do you know?' asked Lauren.

'I don't,' said Jake. 'I'm guessing. But I bet I'm right.'

'So what are we going to do?'

'We go to the police,' said Jake.

# Chapter 7

Jake and Lauren waited for twenty minutes in the police station reception before DI Bullen appeared. He didn't look pleased to see them.

'You needn't have waited to see me,' he said. 'You could have handed in your passport to the desk sergeant.'

'It's not just that we came to see you about,' said Jake. 'It's Guy de Courcey.'

'Oh?'

Bullen's attitude changed immediately. He was suddenly alert. He thinks I've come to shop Guy, thought Jake. Tell him that it was Guy who did the killing, and I was just an innocent accomplice, or something like that.

'He's disappeared,' said Jake.

Bullen looked at Jake, then at Lauren, frowning, puzzled.

'What do you mean, disappeared?' he asked. 'How do you know?'

'Because he asked us to meet him at his hotel at twelve o'clock. The Belvedere. We went there, but the receptionist told us he'd checked out.'

'So?' said Bullen. 'Maybe he did.'

'Do you know about it?' asked Jake. 'Because my guess is that, if he's still a suspect, you'll want to know where he's staying. Or, has he done a runner?'

Bullen's expression tightened.

'Wait here,' he said.

With that, he disappeared through the door that led to the offices and the cells.

They sat back down on the hard plastic chairs, and waited. It was a further twenty minutes before Bullen reappeared, and this time he was more relaxed.

'Everything's in order,' he said. 'We've spoken to Lord de Courcey's solicitors, and they have assured us that they have given him one of their private apartments. They've provided us with the address.'

'And have you checked it to make sure he's there?' asked Jake.

Bullen visibly bridled at Jake telling him how to do his job.

'Why should we?' he demanded.

'Because I had this text,' said Jake, and he showed it to Bullen.

Bullen looked at the word 'hlp'.

'So?'

'I think Guy sent it,' said Jake. 'I think he's asking for help.'

'From *you*?' Then Bullen's tone changed and he asked, 'If this is from him, why would he ask you for help? You said you didn't know him.'

'I didn't, not before last night,' said Jake.

Bullen stood studying Jake, suspicion obvious on his face. Finally, he gave a dismissive shrug and said, 'Anyway, Lord de Courcey isn't in any immediate trouble, apart from being a suspect in this case. As you are. We've just spoken to his solicitors, and they have assured us he is safe.'

'They could be holding him against his will,' said Jake.

'Why would they do that?' asked Bullen.

Because they're criminals, thought Jake. Pierce Randall work with assassins and terrorists. They'd do anything to protect their investments. Kidnapping, torture and killing would be no problem for them.

Aloud, he said, 'Because there's a lot of money at stake here.'

Bullen fixed Jake with a hard glare.

'Pierce Randall are a highly reputable and international firm of solicitors,' he snapped. 'I would think very carefully before making any accusations against them of wrongdoing.' He then gestured towards the reception desk. 'We still need your passport. If it's not delivered to us within the next two hours . . .'

'It's here,' said Jake, taking it from his pocket.

'Hand it in to the desk,' Bullen said brusquely. 'They'll issue you with a receipt for it.' He gave Jake a searching look. 'Anything else?'

Jake hesitated. He wanted to have a go at Bullen, tell him how incompetent he was being in refusing to listen to his concerns about Pierce Randall, ignoring the risks that Guy was facing. But then it struck him that maybe it wasn't incompetence on Bullen's part. Maybe the DI was being paid by Pierce Randall. It still puzzled Jake how he and Guy had been released so easily, especially when they were the prime suspects in a murder case.

'Jake!' said Lauren sharply, sensing Jake's mood. 'Just give them your passport.'

Jake hesitated again, then nodded.

'OK,' he said.

Once they were outside in the street, Lauren turned to Jake, annoyed.

'What were you thinking of?' she demanded. 'You don't want to give him any excuse to take you back in.'

'Guy's been snatched,' said Jake. 'I just wanted Bullen to at least say he'd investigate it.'

'He did,' said Lauren. 'He contacted Pierce Randall, who told him everything was fine.'

'And would you believe Pierce Randall?' asked Jake.

'No,' admitted Lauren. 'Not about anything. But he's right about one thing, you don't know who that text was from.'

'Who else could it be?' demanded Jake.

'It could be from Gareth,' said Lauren thoughtfully.

'Gareth!'

'I told you, his wife sounded very frightened when I spoke to her. She refused to talk to me. She hung up.'

'So? I expect that's what Gareth's told her to do with any phone callers she doesn't know.'

'And we don't know where he is,' Lauren continued. 'He never returned my calls.'

'He's possibly got caught up in some major spy business somewhere,' said Jake. 'Remember, that's what he does. And if it had been Gareth who'd texted me, it would have shown his name. I've got his number in my phone.'

'Good point,' she admitted. 'OK, so the text could be from Guy. So what are we going to do?'

Jake thought it over.

'I'll go and see Gareth tomorrow at the office. See if he can get to the bottom of this.'

'And if Gareth's not there? Say I was right about why his wife sounded frightened?'

Jake fell silent as what Lauren had said finally sunk in. What if she was right? Say something *had* happened to Gareth?

# Chapter 8

The next morning Jake arrived at the offices of the Department of Science in Marsham Street, just a quick dash from the Houses of Parliament at Westminster. The building was a large modernistic glass tower, the glass in various shades of green, aimed at promoting an image of the department as at the forefront of twenty-first-century science, pushing the boundaries for the future. Inside, the main reception area and the first two floors continued that theme: modernistic in design, awash with flat screens and digital technology.

Once you got up to the third floor, however, and only people who worked in the building ever got that high, the interior decor changed. From here upwards it was all very old-fashioned with images of science from the past, along with pictures from Victorian times. Jake had often reflected that the people who ran the department, the decision makers on the top floors, preferred to look backwards to the glories of the past.

Jake's office, the large open-plan press office, was on the first floor of the building, but right now he had something more important on his mind than work, and that was seeing Gareth Findlay-Weston, his boss.

Jake took the lift up to the third floor and made his way along the narrow corridor, hung with oil paintings of hunting scenes. He reached Gareth's office, knocked, and went in.

Gareth's secretary, Janet, was in her usual place, on guard at her desk in the outer office, Gareth's protector and gatekeeper. She was talking quietly and seriously on the phone, but as Jake came in she said, 'I'll talk to you later,' and hung up.

'Hi,' said Jake. 'Is Gareth in? I need to see him urgently.'

Janet seemed to hesitate a second, then she said, 'He's not in.'

'Do you know when he will be in?'

Again, Janet appeared to hesitate. Then she said, 'No.'

Jake looked at her, puzzled.

'Is he *meant* to be in?' he asked. 'I mean, he's not on holiday, or something?'

'No,' said Janet. And, although she was doing her best to stay the perfect calm and efficient secretary

that she always was, Jake was sure there was something not right. She looked nervous. No, not nervous;
upset.

'Is everything all right? asked Jake.

'Yes.'

But her answer was too quick. This wasn't the Janet
that Jake was familiar with. By reputation, Gareth's
secretary, although small in size, was a tough woman
who scared the life out of everyone in the building,
with the exception of Gareth. She was known behind
her back as Gareth's Rottweiler, his fierce guard dog,
one who was capable of great savagery — usually verbal
— if it meant protecting her beloved boss.

There was no sign of the Rottweiler today. Right now,
Janet was nervous, flustered, unhappy. No, *deeply*
unhappy.

'When will he be in?' pressed Jake. 'Only there's
something very important I need to discuss with him.'

Janet hesitated, then she said, 'At the moment he's
on an assignment.'

Jake frowned.

'What sort of assignment?'

'I'm afraid that's classified,' snapped Janet sharply,
a hint of the old Rottweiler surfacing.

'Do you know when he'll be back?'

'It's . . . it's open-ended.'

'So . . . no?'

'I'm sorry,' said Janet, although the tight-lipped look she gave Jake said that she wasn't sorry at all, 'but I have some important work to be getting on with.'

'Of course,' Jake nodded apologetically. 'But, if you're in touch with him, will you give him my message? That I need to see him urgently.'

'Of course.'

With that, Janet turned back to her desk and began sorting through some papers. But Jake felt sure that this activity was just a cover. Something was wrong. Gareth wasn't in, and Janet didn't know why. Or, she *did* know why, and she was frightened because of it.

Jake left Gareth's office and walked back down the stairs to the first floor, and the office where he and the other minions of the Department of Science press office carried out their duties. His friend Paul Evans was just hanging up the phone as he arrived.

'Bloody Area 51,' Paul grumbled.

Jake frowned.

'Area 51?' he repeated. 'In America?'

Paul laughed.

'Not that one,' he chuckled. 'Our very own Area 51. Laker Heath. You know, where all the oddball stuff is kept. Our own flying saucers, aliens, that sort of thing.' He laughed. 'At least, that's what the conspiracy freaks seem to believe.'

Jake shook his head.

73

'No one's told me about this,' he said.

'Oh, come on!' said Paul. 'Remember that time you got caught up in that escape of toxic gas? The hallucinations at that building site. I told you then about Sigma.'

'Sigma?'

'The code they use for all these oddball things. Hoax or hallucination.'

Jake felt a sick feeling inside, wondering if this was going to lead up to Paul talking about the Malichea books. It was a subject he'd always avoided talking about to Paul, or anyone else at work, with the exception of Gareth. And, as far as he knew, no one at press office level, except himself, even knew about the hidden Malichea books; and it wasn't something he wanted to air now.

'Anyway,' said Paul airily, 'you'd be kept out of the loop as far as what goes on at Area 51. You're not cleared. It's Level Five security only. You're still . . . what? Level Three?'

'That's nonsense!' insisted Jake. 'I went on a training course at Laker Heath when I was first here. There was no suggestion there was anything odd about the place.'

'Well, they're hardly likely to admit that to a new trainee,' said Paul.

'Yes, but I had an even lower level security clearance then,' Jake insisted. 'If Laker Heath really is where all those sorts of things are kept . . .'

'Rumoured to be kept,' corrected Paul.

'OK, rumoured,' said Jake. 'The bottom line is that I wouldn't have been allowed in. But I was.'

'Did you go into the hangar?' asked Paul.

Jake frowned.

'What hangar?'

'The large aircraft hangar right at the western end.'

'No,' admitted Jake. 'Our training course was in the main building, near the main gate.'

'There you are, then.' Paul smiled. 'It's inside that hangar that the real stuff is kept.' He winked. 'Alien spacecraft. Monsters from the deep.' Then he sighed and gestured at the phone. 'Which is why whenever anything happens at Laker Heath we get bombarded with reporters chasing some weird story. Like just now.'

'What?' asked Jake, intrigued.

'Someone in the area reported glowing lights hovering over the hangars at the place, so, naturally, they suspected UFOs.'

'And were they?' asked Jake, even more intrigued.

'Oh, please, Jake!' scoffed Paul. 'UFOs, indeed!'

Jake forced a chuckle.

'Just joking,' he said, to cover it up. But, with all the things he'd discovered through the Malichea business, he'd learnt that anything was possible.

'It was a prototype solar-powered weather balloon they were testing,' said Paul. 'But try telling that to these lunatics. As far as they're concerned it's just another cover-up.' Then he said, 'By the way, sorry, but all the talk of Area 51 put it out of my head. There was a call for you while you were out. Switchboard put it through to me.'

'Oh?' asked Jake, 'Who was it?'

'He said his name was Guy,' said Paul.

'Guy?' echoed Jake. Why had Guy phoned him at the office? Why hadn't he called him on his mobile? It didn't make sense. Why should Guy go to all the bother of finding out his number at the Department of Science press office?

'Did he leave a number where I could get hold of him?'

'No. He said he'd try again.'

'How did he sound?'

'What do you mean?' asked Paul, puzzled.

'Well, did he sound nervous? Agitated?'

'No,' said Paul. Then he frowned thoughtfully. 'Actually, he sounded foreign.'

'Foreign?'

Paul nodded.

'He had an accent. It sounded sort of Spanish.'

Spanish? That's not Guy, thought Jake. But why would someone Spanish phone Jake pretending to be Guy?

Changing the subject, Jake asked, 'Have you heard anything about Gareth?'

Paul frowned.

'What in particular?' he asked.

'Well, where he is?' said Jake. 'I've just been up to see him and Janet says he's away.'

'Well, if that's what she says, then I guess that's where he is.' Paul shrugged.

'Yes, but we didn't get a memo saying he was going to be away,' pointed out Jake. 'And usually, if he's away, we get told who to report to in his absence. You know, if anything big comes up and we need to refer it upwards.'

'Why, has something big come up that you know about?' asked Paul.

'Well, no,' said Jake. 'But it might.'

Paul shook his head.

'I'm sure, if anything does happen that needs someone more important than us to handle, you can just pass it up to Janet. She'll know what to do with it. They don't call her the Rottweiler for nothing!' He grinned. 'I don't know about you, but I find her terrifying.'

At the moment, I just feel terrified, thought Jake.


The whole way on the Tube home to Finsbury Park, Jake thought about everything that had happened in the last seventy-two hours. Alex Munro being shot dead. Jake being arrested for his murder, and meeting Guy — now

*Earl* Guy — de Courcey. Guy vanishing. And now Gareth disappearing. And in both disappearances there was an absolute silence: a refusal by anyone to admit that they'd vanished.

And then there had been the phone call from Guy. Or someone pretending to be Guy. Someone who was possibly Spanish.

Maybe the mystery caller had been someone from Guy's recent past in Mexico. But why call Jake?

When he arrived at their flat, Lauren was sitting at her laptop. She got up and gave him a welcoming smile, and he realised that what with all this business with Guy and Gareth it had been ages since they'd spent real time together.

Jake made coffee for them and they shared their day's experiences.

'Did you see Gareth?' asked Lauren.

'He wasn't in the office,' said Jake. 'And I'm pretty sure there's something going on. Something weird. But if he *is* in any kind of trouble, I'm pretty sure that MI5 will already be swinging into action.' He gestured towards Lauren's laptop. 'How did you get on with checking out our missing friend, Guy.'

'You still think it was Guy who texted you?'

'Yes, I do. Call it a hunch, but he's the only person I can think of who'd do it.'

'Even though, according to the police, Pierce Randall say he's safe?'

'*Because* Pierce Randall say he's safe,' said Jake sarcastically. 'So, what did you find out?'

'That the de Courceys are definitely heavily involved in the Malichea books,' said Lauren.

She went to her laptop and began to flick her fingers over the keys. A genealogical family tree appeared on the screen.

'The de Courcey family tree,' she said. She scrolled down until the screen showed a date of 1539. She pointed to two names. 'Edgar de Courcey. He was the librarian of the Order of Malichea from 1536 until 1539.'

'The year that Glastonbury was destroyed and The Index and the *Journal* vanished,' said Jake.

'And Edgar de Courcey died that same year. It wouldn't surprise me to find he was a victim of Henry VIII's purge of the monasteries.' Lauren's finger moved to the other name on the screen. 'Earl William de Courcey, brother of Edgar. Direct ancestor of your cellmate.'

'So it looks like it fits. Edgar de Courcey realises what's about to happen, and gives The Index and the *Journal of the Order of Malichea* to his brother, William, for safe keeping. And the books get put away in the library at de Courcey Hall, right up until . . . when?'

'Until very recently, if I'm right,' said Lauren. 'Earl William died in 1563 and the title continued to be passed on down the line, right up to the present day.'

'Right up to the new earl, our vanished friend, Guy,' murmured Jake.

Lauren nodded.

'According to what I've been able to find out, the family lived in their ancestral home of de Courcey Hall in Kent right up until 2012, when the hall was given to the National Trust by Guy's father — Earl Edwyn de Courcey.'

'Yes, that's what Guy told me.' Jake nodded.

'Shortly afterwards, Earl Edwyn died, and Guy inherited the title,' added Lauren. 'But, as Guy was away at the time, he didn't immediately claim it. It's possible he didn't even know his father was dead. Apparently there was no love lost between Guy and his father.'

She typed in the words 'Guy de Courcey', and selected one of the entries that came up. It was a brief biog telling them that Guy de Courcey was the last surviving member of the de Courcey family, that he was twenty-two years old. Lauren flicked the keys again, and a series of reports came up, mostly from gossip columns. They learnt that Guy had been expelled from his public school, had been arrested on different occasions for smuggling contraband into foreign countries, but had usually been released after 'judicial compensation' had been paid.

'Bribes,' commented Jake. 'He told me his solicitors had paid to have him bailed out, but he also said they weren't the sort who paid bribes.'

'So who did pay them?' asked Lauren. 'He told you he was broke.'

'He told me quite a few things,' said Jake. 'I'm still not sure how true they all were, especially now he's vanished.'

'According to the internet gossip, Guy's last known address was in Brazil,' said Lauren.

'But Pierce Randall traced him to Mexico,' said Jake.

'That's what he told you,' said Lauren. 'We still don't know for sure if he was telling you the truth.'

'Or if Pierce Randall are telling the truth when they say that Guy is safe in their hands,' said Jake. He frowned. 'Know what I think?'

'What?'

'I think we ought to check out Pierce Randall at their HQ.'

'Why?'

'They're the key figures here. Their CEO, Alex Munro, gets shot. They get one of his alleged killers out on bail and hide him away. Whatever's going on, they're the ones who are running things. They're the ones who know what's really happening.'

'And how will that help us?'

'Once we get to the bottom of what's really going on, we'll be able to prove I'm innocent of killing Munro.'

'It's worth a try,' said Lauren.

'It's the only option we've got,' said Jake. 'Do you remember the name of their solicitor who bailed Guy out?'

Lauren shook her head.

'I was only interested in getting you out,' she said. 'We could always ask DI Bullen.'

'And my guess is he'll tell us he's not allowed to pass on information about other individuals,' sighed Jake. Then an idea hit him. 'That solicitor who got me out of custody before!'

'When?'

'When they found that dead body in my flat, when all this started. You know, the solicitor from Pierce Randall who arrived at the police station and got me out. What was her name?' He frowned, struggling to remember.

Lauren shook her head.

'I didn't know anything about her. I had troubles of my own.' She shuddered at her own memory of those times.

'Sue Clark!' he burst out. 'That was her name!' He picked up his mobile and began searching the listings for Pierce Randall's phone number.

'What are you going to ask her?'

'I'm going to ask if she can arrange for us to see Guy.'

'Why?'

'Because, like I said, I think he's in trouble. Either Pierce Randall are keeping him prisoner, or someone else is.'

'In which case, we won't be able to see Guy.'

'And then we'll know for sure he's being held against his will.'

'Or maybe they just want him kept away from us.'

Jake shrugged. 'Maybe. But at least we'll get some idea of what's really going on.'

'Only if she agrees to see us,' said Lauren.

'She'll see us,' said Jake grimly. 'I'm going to make her an offer she can't refuse.'

The young man hung up his phone. So, Jake Wells and Lauren Graham were on the move. Pierce Randall was their next stop. Good. Things were moving, but not as fast as he would have liked. It was time to step the game up a gear. To move on from just tracking them, hunting them, watching as they made the moves he wanted them to make. It was time to give them a push towards the edge. Then, when they'd delivered, he could kick them over that edge. Dead.

He wondered about Gareth Findlay-Weston. It had been a bold move on his part, the right move to make, but had it got him any further towards his goal?

Jake remembered when he'd last been here, over a year ago. Then, he'd been brought to meet Alex Munro for the first time and had been offered the chance to work in partnership with the law firm to recover the hidden books. Munro had appeared sincere, genuine, even caring. As Jake was to discover later, that had all been a front. The only things that Pierce Randall cared about were money and power. That was how they'd built up their financial empire. For them, the hidden books of Malichea represented both money *and* power. That was why Jake was dangling the offer of one in front of them now.

A tall man in a neat dark suit approached them.

'Mr Wells? Ms Graham?' he asked politely.

'Yes.' Jake and Lauren stood up.

'My name's James. I am Ms Clark's personal assistant. I'm to take you up to see her, if you'll follow me.'

Jake and Lauren exchanged nervous looks as they followed the tall man towards the security gates. This was it!

James swiped his pass through a security scanner, and kept the gate open while Jake and Lauren came through. He then headed towards the lifts.

The journey up in the lift was fast and smooth. They stopped at the fifteenth floor, and followed James along a plushly carpeted corridor to a glass-walled office. He tapped at the door and announced, 'Mr Wells and Ms Graham, Ms Clark.'

'Thank you, James,' said Clark.

Sue Clark hadn't changed much since Jake had last seen her, when she'd sprung him from a police interrogation room and a charge of murder. She was a woman in her mid-twenties, wearing a smart and expensive-looking charcoal-grey suit, and with a look of intense anger in her eyes, barely hidden beneath her stern expression.

Clark indicated the two chairs on the other side of the desk, and Jake and Lauren sat down as James left.

'On the phone you said you had one of the books to offer,' said Clark.

'Straight down to business?' queried Jake. 'No social niceties?'

'You are accused of killing someone who was very important to this firm, and to me personally,' said Clark curtly. 'I have no wish for us to be friends.' She turned to Lauren and added, 'You and I have never met, Ms Graham, but I have heard a lot about you. Anyone who can do what you did and get away with it is someone who deserves some kind of respect.'

The sneering way that Clark said it made Lauren feel anger rising inside her. Jake was obviously aware of her reaction, because he reached out a hand and rested it on Lauren's thigh, warning her to stay calm.

Clark turned back to Jake and said curtly, 'Now we've got the social niceties out of the way, can we get down to why you're here. You said you have a book to offer us. Why, when you've spent all your energies so far opposing us getting hold of them?'

'Because I'm charged with murder,' said Jake. 'The books will be no use to me if I'm in prison.'

'You want us to represent you?'

'Perhaps,' said Jake. 'But right now we need to see Guy de Courcey, and we'd like you to arrange that.'

Clark shook her head.

'We've advised Lord de Courcey not to have any contact with you.'

'Why?'

'Because you are both accused of Alex Munro's murder, with the suggestion of conspiracy. In our opinion, contact with you could compromise his position in this case. We think it best if you and he remain separate.'

'What if I became your client?' asked Jake.

'Why would we want to take on your case?' countered Clark.

'You've always said you wanted to work with me before,' Jake pointed out.

'That was different,' said Clark. Then she added carefully, 'Unless you really have got one of the books to offer.'

'You don't trust me?' asked Jake. 'You think I'm lying about the book?'

'I've got an open mind on the question,' said Clark. 'However, I do keep asking myself: why would you suddenly offer me the book?'

'I've already told you, I've got a murder charge hanging over me,' replied Jake.

'And, if you really have got hold of one of the books, why haven't you put it out into the public domain, as you both have said you wanted to do with the books?' added Clark.

'Because our experiences have taught us to be very careful,' put in Lauren quickly. 'We still don't know who we can trust.'

'And suddenly you've decided you can trust us?' queried Clark suspiciously.

'No,' admitted Jake. 'But right now I'm in deep trouble, and using the book as a bargaining chip is the best way of getting out of it.' He shrugged. 'There are other books.'

Clark studied Jake's face carefully, trying to see if he was lying.

'We'd need to have sight of the book first,' she said.

Jake shook his head.

'Oh no,' he said. 'The last time I handed over one of the books to you, it was taken off me and I was thrown out of the building with nothing.'

Clark fell silent again, and Jake could almost see her mind whirring and working.

'We'd need some kind of proof from you, first,' she said. 'You could be bluffing.'

'What about a photograph?' suggested Lauren.

'A photograph?'

'A film, even better,' continued Lauren. 'We record us holding the book, and then opening the first page so you can get a look at it.'

'And then what?' asked Clark.

'You let us meet Guy, and you sign the necessary paperwork to say you'll represent Jake in this case, and we'll hand the book over to you.'

'As easily as that?' queried Clark, her voice filled with disbelief.

'Do I have to say it again? I've got a murder charge hanging over me,' said Jake. 'The book will be no use to me if I end up in prison.'

Clark fell silent again. Obviously she hadn't expected this offer.

Finally, she said, 'I'll have to take this up with the senior partners. As I've said, Lord de Courcey is in a very secure and protected environment, for his own safety, and the senior partners will need to be persuaded it's in our firm's interests to let you see him.'

'Tell them about our offer,' said Jake. 'One of the lost books of Malichea.'

'With the photograph and the video as proof,' reminded Lauren.

'Very well,' said Clark. 'I'll pass that on to them. And you'll hear from me shortly.'

# Chapter 10

As Jake and Lauren left the building, Jake whispered, 'Are you crazy?'

'What?' asked Lauren.

'That offer of videoing us with one of the books! I was just going to offer her the *idea* of a book!'

Lauren shrugged. 'She didn't believe you. We needed to show her some proof.'

'But we don't have one of the books to film!'

'No problem. We said we'd only show them the cover, and the first page. We fake one. We've seen the books before, we know what they look like. They're not going to be able to examine it up close.'

'They'll want to once we've talked to Guy.'

'So, we tell them we don't have it.'

'That we lied to them?'

Lauren shrugged again. 'Pierce Randall make their living by lying. It's what they do. This way they'll be getting a taste of their own medicine.'

'Lauren, Pierce Randall kill people who cheat them.'

Lauren scowled deeply.

'That woman annoyed me! The way she treated me! I wanted to wipe that smug look off her face by giving her something to think about. Anyway, are you satisfied now?'

'About the fact we could end up dead?'

'About Guy,' said Lauren. 'She said she'd be able to fix up a meeting with him.'

'From his "secure and protected environment",' quoted Jake. 'That sounds like he's a prisoner to me.'

'Yes, but he's in their hands, not anyone else's.'

They headed towards the nearest underground station. They were just nearing the entrance when a man stepped in their path.

'Stop,' he said curtly.

Lauren saw the glint of metal in the man's hand.

'Jake, he's got a knife!' she whispered.

'Where is Guy de Courcey?' demanded the man, and now Jake could hear his accent, a very guttural Spanish.

'Guy?' he echoed.

'Do not try to run!' snapped the man. 'My men are right behind you.'

Jake looked round, and saw a very tall, muscular man standing behind them. One of his hands was in his pocket, the other bunched into a fist.

Jake turned back.

'Look, we don't know where Guy de Courcey is . . .'
he began.

The man scowled.

'I do not believe you!' He gestured back along the road. 'You have just been to Pierce Randall.'

'Yes, but . . .' began Jake.

The man glared at him.

'Get in the van!' he snapped.

'Van?'

Parked on the kerb was a small van with 'HO Rentals' painted on the side. A third man was sitting behind the steering wheel.

'Listen,' Jake said, angrily. 'I don't know what you think . . .'

'Get in the van!' repeated the man, his voice angrier this time. He pointed the knife towards Lauren. 'And no shouting or she die.'

'Look, we don't know where Guy de Courcey is . . .' protested Jake.

The man moved towards Lauren and placed the blade of his knife near her stomach.

'OK,' said Jake quickly.

Jake and Lauren climbed into the back of the van. There were no seats inside, just the bare metal of the floor. The two men climbed in after them and pulled the van doors shut. The leader said something in Spanish to the driver, and the van pulled away.

'Listen,' Jake appealed again, 'neither of us know where Guy de Courcey is. We're guessing you know him, otherwise you wouldn't be doing this. But we'd never met him, or even heard about him, until the other day.'

'Jake Wells?' asked the man suspiciously.

'Yes,' admitted Jake.

'Guy said he coming to England to meet you.'

'You're from Mexico!' said Lauren with a burst of sudden realisation. She turned to Jake. 'Remember, Guy told you he was in Mexico when Pierce Randall contacted him.'

'Shh!' snapped the man. He turned back to Jake. 'Guy said he come to England to see Jake Wells and Alex Munro. Now Munro dead and Guy vanish. What you do with him?'

'I haven't done anything with him!' said Jake, exasperated. 'I didn't do anything with either of them! Like I told you, I'd never even *heard* of Guy de Courcey before we were both locked up in the same cell by the police.' Then he added, in the hope it might worry the men, 'Who might even be tailing us, for all we know.'

The man ignored this, and insisted, 'You lie. You know Guy before.'

'No!' said Jake.

The man turned to Lauren.

'You know him?'

95

'No!' said Lauren defensively.

The man scowled, and muttered something in Spanish to one of the others.

'*Sí*,' grunted the second man, and he took a vicious-looking metal knuckleduster from his pocket and slipped it on the fingers of his huge right fist.

'My friend going to break the bones in your face until you tell us where Guy is.' He gestured to Lauren. 'He start with her. He hurt her real bad.'

'Look, if we knew where Guy was, we'd tell you!' appealed Jake. 'We don't know! We went to the hotel where he told us he was staying . . .'

'The Belvedere, *sí*.'

'And he'd left. We got the impression he was being taken care of by the firm of lawyers that Alex Munro worked for, Pierce Randall. They're the people you should be talking to.'

'We talk to them. They say they don't know.'

'And neither do we!'

Suddenly the van braked hard, throwing them all off balance. Jake jerked forward, grabbed the man's hand holding the knife and slammed it down hard. The man screamed as the blade sliced into his leg.

At the same time, Lauren swung her right hand up, bringing the heel of her hand sharply up under the nose of the man nearest her, snapping it and sending him reeling backwards with a yell of pain.

Jake slid across the floor of the van and kicked out hard at the rear doors. They sprang open. There was the blare of a horn as the vehicle immediately behind the van braked sharply. Jake and Lauren dived out, dodging through the traffic as they ran for the pavement. They threw themselves into the mass of people and darted into a side street, and then another, before finally stopping, out of breath.

They looked back. There was no sign of the Mexicans.

'They don't need to chase us,' said Lauren. 'If they know your name, they'll know where we live.'

'Yes, but next time we'll be on our guard,' said Jake. 'And I'm hoping that we proved back there that we can't be bullied.'

# Chapter 11

Their Tube journey home was spent in silence. Both Jake and Lauren knew it was not a good idea to start talking about what had happened to them in a train where their conversation could be overheard by other passengers. To talk about almost being abducted, and Mexicans with knives, could easily raise alarm. At the same time, neither of them felt at ease enough to engage in idle chatter about everyday things. As they exited Finsbury Park station, it was Lauren who spoke first, cutting off Jake.

'We have to tell the police!'

'I'm not sure that's a good idea,' argued Jake. 'Bullen seems convinced that I'm playing games with him. He'll just think I'm doing the same again, and haul me in.'

'But we have evidence! The van! OH Rentals. Descriptions of the three men!'

Jake frowned.

'I'm still not sure. What I don't understand is this business of Guy telling them he was coming to England to meet me.'

'Maybe Alex Munro told him that was what was going to happen. Your name was in Munro's diary, remember.'

'But why didn't Munro contact me?'

Lauren shrugged.

'Who knows?' She shuddered. 'One thing's for sure, Guy certainly mixed with some rough people in Mexico.'

'He told me he was in prison there,' said Jake. 'Let's hope there aren't any more of his former cellmates walking around looking for him.'

'What I don't get is: why us?' asked Lauren.

'Because they think I'm connected to Guy in some way,' said Jake. 'Someone with a Spanish accent phoned me at the office before we went to see Sue Clark. He claimed to be Guy.'

'You never told me!' said Lauren accusingly. 'What did you say to him?'

'I never got the chance to tell you about him, what with everything else going on. Anyway, I never spoke to him. Paul took the message.'

'What worries me is, they'll try again,' said Lauren.

'Maybe we really do need Pierce Randall on our side,' Jake suggested. 'I bet they know exactly what's going on. Guy and Gareth missing. Everything that's behind it. They always know.'

Lauren shook her head.

'They won't help us unless we give them the book, like we promised. And once they find out we forged it, they'll . . .'

'Kill us?' said Jake.

'Don't joke about it,' said Lauren.

'Who said I was joking?' snapped Jake bitterly.

'There's no need to have a go at me!' retorted Lauren, stung.

'I wasn't!'

'Yes, you were!'

Jake was about to snap back at her, when he stopped himself.

'OK, it sounded like it, but I didn't mean to,' he said apologetically. 'It's just that . . . after what happened . . .'

'Whatever's going on, one thing's for sure: Pierce Randall can't be trusted,' said Lauren grimly. 'We know they're only in this for what they can get out of it. If we want Pierce Randall, or anyone else, on our side, we need a bargaining chip. We really do need a book.'

Jake turned to Lauren, his face alight with inspiration.

'No, we need *the* book!' he said. 'The Index! The reason Pierce Randall brought Guy back! That's what this is all about!'

Lauren sighed.

'We don't know where The Index is. *No one* knows where The Index is.'

Jake smiled at her.

'I think I do! It just hit me!'

Again, Lauren shook her head.

'You're dreaming, Jake,' she said. 'If The Index was that easy to find, Pierce Randall would have got hold of it by now. Or Gareth and MI5. Or every other organisation who've been looking for it.'

'I've been thinking about that,' said Jake. 'Ever since I met Guy and heard his story. And the answer's only just hit me right now. Why did Pierce Randall bring Guy back to England?'

'Because, like we said, his ancestor was quite likely given the *Journal*, and possibly The Index, for safe keeping.'

'And where would those books have been kept?'

Lauren stared at him.

'Jake, you're not seriously suggesting . . .'

'Yes, I am! In the library at de Courcey Hall in Kent.'

'But the National Trust would have cleared the library out.'

'Not necessarily. Have you ever noticed that in lots of these National Trust places, the libraries are still filled with old books that look as if they've been there for centuries?' said Jake. 'Say that was the case here.'

'My God!' breathed Lauren. 'If it *is* . . .' She looked stunned. 'You surely don't think it can be that simple? That The Index and the *Journal* could have been sitting there on the library shelves at de Courcey Hall all this time?'

'It's possible.'

'But if The Index has been there all this time, why would Pierce Randall need Guy to get it? They're powerful enough to be able to get it without him.'

'Perhaps Pierce Randall has already searched the library but couldn't find it. Plus, they probably don't know what it looks like. Guy lived at the place. I reckon that they thought he might be able to pinpoint it for them. There could be a hidden compartment in the library that Guy might remember from childhood?'

'So you think The Index might still be there at the hall?'

'There's only one way to find out,' said Jake.

# Chapter 12

As Jake and Lauren drove along the narrow winding lane that led to de Courcey Hall, Jake was desperate to believe this trip would lead them finally to the end of their long and painful quest. The Index, the list of places where every one of the Malichea books was hidden.

The car followed the twists and turns, until they rounded a final bend and saw the hall ahead of them.

It was massive. OK, not as big as somewhere like Buckingham Palace, and it wasn't many storeys high, like some stately homes, but it was a rambling Tudor mansion with additional wings, all in the same black timber-framed style bending this way and that.

'Wow!' said Jake. 'That is some house! It looks like it's got . . . what . . . a hundred rooms? And one family lived here?'

'Plus their servants. And guest wings for important visitors. Royalty arriving with all their attendants and servants. A place like this needed to be big.'

They drove past a single-storey gatehouse towards the car park.

'It's huge!' murmured Jake. 'It must have cost a fortune to maintain this place!'

'It still looks like it did way back in Tudor times,' said Lauren, bringing up an image of an old painting of the house on her iPhone.

'Let's hope the library is still the same,' said Jake.

He followed the signs for the car park. There were just two cars already there, and an SUV.

'Not many visitors,' he remarked.

'Damn!' muttered Lauren.

'What?'

She pointed to a sign that read: 'Public opening hours: 11 a.m. to 4 p.m.'

'Half past nine,' she said, her voice showing how fed up she was. 'We've got an hour and a half to wait.'

'Maybe they'll let us in early?'

'On what grounds?'

'We don't actually want to see the whole house, just check out the library.'

'So?'

'We tell them we're doing some research on a historical project about the library. Flash them your British Library card. That'll impress them.'

'It's worth a try, I suppose,' said Lauren. 'They can only say no.'

She had opened the door and was just about to get out, when she let out a gasp of shock and pulled the door shut again.

'What's up?' asked Jake.

'Look!' she said.

Jake followed her gaze, and let out a gasp himself. Guy was walking across the car park, and behind him was a teenage boy of about fifteen, wearing tracksuit bottoms and a hoodie. Even from this distance they could see he was pointing a gun at Guy's back.

'Let's go!' said Jake urgently.

He was just about to open the door and jump out, when Lauren stopped him.

'Are you mad?' she demanded. 'He's got a gun!'

'But . . . It's Guy! In trouble! Just like we said!'

'He won't shoot him,' said Lauren. 'Not here. Not unless you do something stupid.'

'So what do you suggest?'

Guy and the kid reached the SUV. The rear door opened and Guy got inside. Then the kid with the gun got into the front passenger seat.

'There are people already in it,' said Lauren. 'Two in the front, one in the back with Guy. And I bet you the one in the back's also armed.'

'Think I should ram their car?' asked Jake. 'Stop them getting away?'

'And then they shoot us and take our car instead,' said Lauren scornfully. 'No, that'd be suicide. I don't think they've spotted us, so we'll follow them. And I'll phone the police while we're doing it.'

'All right.'

The SUV reversed out of its parking space and headed for the exit. Jake set off after it.

'Not too close,' warned Lauren. 'We don't want to spook them.'

'Yes, OK, I have been here before!' Jake snapped back.

The SUV was a black Ford, and the number plate had been obscured with mud so it was impossible to read it. Jake kept a safe distance from them, while Lauren dialled 999 on her phone. As soon as the emergency services answered, she asked for the police, and told them what was happening.

'What did they say?' asked Jake as Lauren hung up.

'They told me we shouldn't get involved but should leave it to the police.'

'Did they say what they were going to do? Put up roadblocks?'

'No,' said Lauren. She scowled. 'I think she thought it was a hoax call.'

Ahead of them, the SUV had speeded up.

'Let them go,' urged Lauren. 'Otherwise they'll realise we're following them.'

'I don't want to get too far behind,' countered Jake. 'It's OK at the moment while we're on this lane, but once we get to the main road, anything could happen.'

'Hopefully, by then, the police will have turned up,' said Lauren.

Suddenly something made Jake look into his rear-view mirror, and he was shocked to see a car speeding towards them from behind.

'What the hell . . . !' he exclaimed.

The car behind him pulled out, as if trying to overtake.

'What's that lunatic doing!' shouted Jake.

The road was too narrow for two cars to pass, it was almost single track, but the car behind them was definitely trying to overtake. It shot forward, and the next second it was level with Jake and Lauren's Mini. There was a terrible screeching sound as the side of the car scraped the metal of theirs. Then, the other driver swung towards Jake, smashing into his offside and pushing their Mini Cooper towards the nearside of the road.

Jake struggled to save their car, grimly trying to take control of the steering and keep the Mini on the road, but the smash had sent the wheels into a skid, and Jake felt the car slide, and plough through the thick bushes in the verge. As he slammed on the brakes, it stopped short just before it hit a tree.

The car that had forced them off the road had hurtled away at speed, and both it and the SUV were disappearing off round a bend in the road.

Their Mini had stalled. Jake restarted it, and tried to reverse, but the car had got caught up in the thick bushes.

Jake cursed and slammed his fist on to the dashboard.

'That was deliberate,' said Lauren. 'The number plate was covered up with mud, the same as the SUV that had Guy in.'

'But why force us off the road?' demanded Jake.

'They knew who we were. They recognised us.'

'But we never got out of the car!'

'So they knew who we were from our car registration.'

'But who . . . ?' began Jake. And then the obvious answer hit him, and both he and Lauren said it at the same time: 'Pierce Randall.'

'Anyway, with any luck the police will have stopped them,' said Jake.

Lauren was already dialling 999 on her phone. Once again, she got through to the police emergency operator, and reported what had happened.

'What did they say?' asked Jake.

'She said a patrol car was already on its way to de Courcey Hall,' she said. 'She told us to wait here for it.'

'Looks like we don't have much of a choice,' groaned Jake resignedly. 'They'll be well clear by now.'

'Hopefully the police will have more luck spotting two cars travelling in convoy,' she said. 'Especially with both of them having hidden number plates.'

'That won't be the case for long,' said Jake gloomily. 'Pierce Randall aren't stupid. Now they've lost us, they'll separate. I bet they even knock the mud off the plates.'

The police patrol car arrived fifteen minutes later, by which time Jake had managed to get their car back on to the verge. It was badly dented, and the front offside headlamp was broken, but it was driveable.

While one of the police officers talked to Jake and Lauren, the other walked around their car, making a note of the damage. Then, when she'd done that, she produced a breathalyser kit and asked Jake to blow into it.

'I'm not drunk!' protested Jake. 'Someone forced us off the road!'

'Then you won't mind breathing into the tube, will you, sir,' said the policewomen, her tone flat and bland.

Jake sighed in frustration, but breathed into the tube. The police officer took it and examined the digital display, made a note in her notebook, then returned the breathalyser to the patrol car. Her colleague checked his own notebook and the statement he'd just taken.

'Let's make sure I've got this right,' he said. 'You say you were following this car because a teenage boy with a gun had forced another man into it . . .'

'And they're getting away!' snapped Jake. 'Didn't you set up road blocks, or anything?'

'And you were following this car, and then a second car came up behind you and forced you off the road.'

'Yes!' said Jake impatiently. 'That's exactly what happened!'

'But you can't give us a description of either of the cars . . .'

'We've given you a description!' said Lauren. 'The first one was a black Ford SUV, and the second one was also black, but everything happened too fast for me to see what make of car it was.'

'But you didn't get the registration numbers of either vehicle.'

'Because the number plates had been smeared with mud, so they couldn't be seen!' retorted Jake in frustration. 'We've told you that already!'

The two police officers exchanged looks.

They don't believe us, realised Jake.

'Why would we be making this up!' he demanded angrily.

'Possibly to try and explain the accident to your car,' said the policewoman.

'It wasn't my fault, if that's what you're suggesting!' burst out Jake angrily.

Just then, the policewoman's radio crackled, and she moved away to listen to a message that was coming in. Her colleague carried on looking at Jake and Lauren, and although the policeman's face remained expressionless, Jake's heart sank as he realised that this was going nowhere.

The policewoman rejoined them.

'Can I just confirm that you are Mr Jacob Wells?' she said to Jake.

'You know I am,' said Jake. 'I showed you my driving licence when you asked me, right at the start when you got here.'

'I've been told to advise you to report to Holloway Road police station immediately,' she said. 'I must advise you that failure to do so could result in a warrant being issued for your arrest.'

'But what about the man in the car? Guy de Courcey! He was being abducted at gunpoint! What about us being run off the road!'

'Our colleagues at Holloway Road will be dealing with those issues,' said the policewoman.

'This is crazy!' said Lauren. 'A man's life is in danger . . .'

'As I said, our colleagues at Holloway Road will be dealing with those issues once you report there,' repeated the policewoman. 'And I would advise you to get there as soon as you can.'

The male police officer gestured to the broken head-lamp on Jake and Lauren's car.

'I would also advise you to get that fixed as soon as possible,' he said. 'Driving a car in that condition is an offence.' He pulled out a small notepad, and filled in a form, which he tore off from the pad and handed to Jake. 'This is an official notice under the Traffic Act ordering you to have that fixed within forty-eight hours.'

Jake looked at the form. On it he'd written their car registration number, the date, and details about the broken headlight.

'I don't believe this!' Jake burst out angrily. 'A man has been kidnapped at gunpoint, and you're giving me a traffic ticket!'

'Our colleagues at Holloway Road station will deal with any other issues,' said the policewoman.

With that, the two officers walked to their patrol car, got in and drove away.

'I don't believe it!' repeated Jake. He screwed up the traffic citation and threw it away at the moving police car.

Beside him, Lauren sighed.

'Better watch out they don't come back and nick you for littering,' she said.

Jake scowled. He knew Lauren was cracking a joke to try to make him feel better, but he was so angry he didn't feel like laughing.

'What now?' he muttered.

'I guess we head back to Holloway Road.' In a hopeful voice, she added, 'Who knows? Maybe they've got news about Guy?'

# Chapter 13

The gridlock of traffic on the M25 was such that it was over two hours before Jake and Lauren finally arrived at Holloway Road police station. There, the desk sergeant put in a call, and Detective Inspector Bullen appeared in reception. He glared at them, and gestured for them to follow him. They walked along the corridor to the same interview room where Bullen had questioned Jake before. This time, though, there was no official caution; no tape running; no other accompanying officers. Bullen pointed at two chairs side by side at a table. Jake and Lauren sat down, and Bullen took a chair opposite. The detective inspector still hadn't said anything and now he spoke, his tone a mixture of anger and frustration.

'What the hell is your game?' he demanded.

'It's no game!' protested Lauren. 'We saw Guy de Courcey being put into a car at gunpoint . . .'

'And you gave chase and then were run off the road by some mystery car,' said Bullen curtly. 'Yes, I know. I got the report through from Kent.'

'Then why aren't you out searching for him?' demanded Jake. 'Why drag us in like we're the culprits?'

'I don't need to search for Lord Guy de Courcey,' said Bullen grimly. 'I know exactly where he is. Or, rather, where he was an hour ago.'

'Where?' asked Lauren.

'He was at Bromley police station in south London, talking to me on the telephone,' said Bullen. 'He'd gone there with his legal representative, to his nearest police station, at my request, as soon as I received word of the allegations you were making.'

Jake and Lauren stared at the detective inspector, stunned.

'But . . .' began Jake.

'There are no "buts",' said Bullen firmly. 'All this talk about him being kidnapped by gunmen is a load of eyewash. Lord de Courcey told us that he was in no danger of any sort.'

'But . . . but,' stammered Jake.

'He was at de Courcey Hall!' exploded Lauren. 'We can prove it! Check the CCTV cameras there!'

'He's quite happy to admit that he was at de Courcey Hall today, but not under duress. He went with his solicitors to see someone he knew, an old friend of the family, who'd agreed to be a character witness for him. De Courcey Hall was a convenient place for them to meet. As his visit wouldn't be in breach of his bail conditions, his solicitors were happy to take him. That's it. End of story.'

'Whoever he was with, they weren't solicitors!' snapped Jake. 'Not unless solicitors are walking around wearing hoodies and tracksuits!'

'And then there were the Mexicans!' burst out Lauren.

'Mexicans?' queried Bullen.

'They took us prisoner and threatened to kill us unless we told them where Guy was!'

'When was this?' demanded Bullen.

'Yesterday,' said Lauren.

'And you've decided to tell us this now?' asked Bullen, his voice heavy with sarcasm.

'We wanted to get hold of The Index first,' said Jake. 'That's why we went to de Courcey Hall.'

Bullen glowered at them.

'That's enough from you two!' he growled. 'I don't know what your game is, but right now I could have you both thrown into the cells and charged with wasting police time. But I choose not to, because I have more important things to do, like solving the murder of Alex Munro. You, Mr Wells, should be treading very carefully.'

'I didn't kill him!' protested Jake. 'I'm innocent!'

'Well, you've got a funny way of showing it. Stunts like this, it's almost like you want to keep reminding me you're here. What is it? Some sort of psychological game? Playing with the police?'

'No!'

Bullen shook his head, his face grim.

'I haven't got time for this. You're lucky I don't lock you up for wasting police time. Now get out!'

The man smiled to himself. It was working perfectly. Jake and Lauren were running around like headless chickens, getting themselves into all sorts of trouble. And all the time their credibility was being destroyed. As far as the police were concerned, the finger of suspicion was pointing even more firmly at Jake. Excellent. Now all he had to do was draw them in, like a spider pulling a fly into its web.

The problem was, they seemed no nearer to finding The Index, and his plan depended on them being pushed by desperation on to its trail, with him following in the shadows, ready to pounce.

Perhaps they needed a bit more of a push.

In the meantime, there was another trail to follow, one he should have thought of before, and he kicked himself mentally for not having thought of it sooner. He had to make a move on that.

'Maybe that's because he had a gun on him,' said Lauren.

'Yes, but if they'd found The Index at de Courcey Hall, Pierce Randall wouldn't have any more use for Guy. So they'd either turn him loose, or bump him off. Yet, instead, they turned up with him at the police station; still keeping a tight hold on him.'

'So you don't think they've got The Index yet?'

'Call it a gut feeling.'

'In which case, if it isn't at the hall, where is it?' asked Lauren.

Jake fell silent, thinking hard. There was something nudging at the back of his mind, a memory, something Guy had said when they were in the cell together. Suddenly he remembered what it was, and he burst out excitedly, 'Hapgood, Ainsworth and Ainsworth!'

Lauren looked at him, baffled.

'Who?' she asked. 'That sounds like a firm of solicitors.'

'That's exactly who they are!' cried Jake. 'They're Guy's solicitors. Or, at least, his solicitors before Pierce Randall. They're the de Courcey *family* solicitors!'

'I still don't get it,' said Lauren, frowning.

'When we were in the cell, Guy told me that his father had sold everything to clear the family's debts.'

'I thought you said the place was *given* to the National Trust.'

# Chapter 14

building that housed the firm of Hapgood, Ainsworth
Ainsworth, of Sevenoaks in Kent, looked as if it
been there for 500 years; and possibly housing that
firm of solicitors during all that time.

ke held open the door and Lauren stepped in,
ght into the sound of raised voices. Or, rather, one
d voice, that of a girl of about fifteen, while the
woman she was talking to tried to calm her down.

on't be put off!' shouted the girl. 'I want to see
sworth!'

I've told you that Mr Ainsworth is busy,' said the
, clearly the receptionist. She turned to Jake
uren and said, 'Yes? Can I help you?'

en Graham and Jake Wells,' said Lauren. 'We
appointment with Mr Ainsworth.'

de Courcey Hall,' added Jake. 'We spoke on
e.'

'It was.' Jake nodded. 'So what was likely
been sold?'

'Paintings?'

Jake shook his head.

'I bet they're still at the hall,' he said.
ings are usually part of the history that g
place. Portraits of the family, that kind o

Lauren looked at Jake, her face fillin
ment at the implication of what Jake w

'The books in the library!' she said.

'The old and rare books, anyway,'
Guy wouldn't have known which boo
because he was out of the country a

'So how do we find out?'

Jake had his iPhone out and wa
the internet as he said, 'We have a
Ainsworth and Ainsworth.'

Th
and
had
sam
Ja
strai
raise
older
'I w
Mr Ain
'And
woman
and La
'Laur
have an
'Abou
the phor

Before the receptionist could reply, the young girl turned to Jake and Lauren and burst out angrily, 'They're a bunch of crooks, all of them! And this lot are as bad, protecting them!'

The woman's face tightened.

'I'm afraid I must ask you to leave, or I will call the police,' she said.

'Call them!' challenged the girl. 'It's about time the police investigated what's going on!'

'That kind of talk is slander,' said the woman primly. 'And saying it in front of witnesses could land you in serious trouble. *Very* serious trouble.'

The girl glared back. She seemed to be on the point of saying something, but instead she scowled, turned on her heel and stormed out, slamming the door shut behind her.

'I'm sorry about that,' said the receptionist.

'Who was she?' asked Jake, intrigued. The girl obviously had some involvement with the hall.

'I'm afraid she's just a disturbed young woman with an imagined grievance.'

The woman pressed a button on the intercom on her desk, and announced, 'Mr Ainsworth. It's Mr Wells and Ms Graham to see you.'

'Thank you, Mrs Ward,' Jake and Lauren heard the man's voice say. 'Please send them up.'

Mrs Ward clicked off the intercom and gestured

towards a flight of stairs at the back of the small reception area.

'First floor,' she said. 'Mr Ainsworth will be waiting for you.'

Jake and Lauren mounted the dark wooden stairs that seemed to be as old as the rest of the building, with the same unevenness. A man in his fifties was waiting for them at the top of the landing, and he shook their hands, and then ushered them into his small office.

'You said on the phone this was about the de Courcey estate,' he said. 'Are you involved in some way with the estate?'

'Possibly,' said Jake. 'We're here following a meeting we had with Guy de Courcey.'

'Ah yes, Mr Guy. Or, as he is now, Lord de Courcey, the new earl.' Ainsworth nodded. 'I must admit I had been disappointed not to have heard from him since he returned to the UK.'

'You mean he hasn't been in touch with you at all?' pressed Lauren.

Ainsworth shook his head.

'In fact, I wouldn't have even known he was back in the country if it wasn't for the fact that a firm called Pierce Randall contacted me to advise me that he was transferring his personal business to them.'

'That must have been disappointing for you,' said Lauren sympathetically.

Ainsworth looked at her quizzically.

'Possibly,' he said. 'Although it has to be said that representing Mr Guy has sometimes been quite . . . involving.'

'Like getting him out of foreign prisons.' Jake grinned.

If he'd hoped this would warm the solicitor towards them, Jake was mistaken. Instead, Ainsworth gave Jake a cold, disapproving look.

'I'm not at liberty to discuss personal details about our clients,' he said sharply.

'No, of course not,' said Jake quickly. 'I apologise. It's just that when I met Guy, he was very happy to tell me about his exploits abroad, and how you'd got him out of various scrapes.'

'Did he,' said Ainsworth, his tone neutral. 'Might I ask the circumstances in which you met Mr Guy?'

As Jake could already feel Ainsworth's disapproval after his attempt at jokey banter, he decided it would be best not to tell the solicitor that he and Guy had met in a police cell, accused of conspiring to murder someone. Instead, he said, 'Oh, just socially.'

'If it *is* about Mr Guy you've come to see me, I must repeat that I'm not at liberty to divulge any details . . .'

'No, no,' said Lauren, nodding. 'It's actually about the library at de Courcey Hall.'

'The library?'

'Yes. Or, rather, the books in it. Guy told us that just before his father gave the house to the National Trust, he sold some of the books in the library.'

'I'm afraid I can't tell you anything about the sale of any of the contents of de Courcey Hall. Or, even, if any such sales took place. Client confidentiality, you understand.'

'Yes, we understand that,' said Lauren. 'But it's not the details of the sale, as far as it affects the de Courcey family, that we're after. It's a particular book we're trying to trace.'

'Oh?'

'Yes. Two books. The *Journal of the Order of Malichea*, and The Index of the same Order. We believe they were in the library of de Courcey Hall.'

Ainsworth shook his head.

'I'm very sorry, but, as I said, due to client confidentiality I can't give you any details of any items sold. However, I am still the solicitor for the estate. I will endeavour to contact the current earl and ask for his permission to speak to you.'

'I don't think Guy is in much of a position to talk freely at the moment,' commented Jake with a sigh.

Ainsworth frowned.

'Why do you say that?' he asked.

Jake caught Lauren's eye, and her slight but meaningful shake of the head, and her lips closing tightly.

Jake shrugged.

'I just meant that I imagine he's pretty busy at the moment. However, if you *do* talk to him, we would be grateful if you'd pass on our message.'

Outside on the street, Jake let out a heartfelt groan.

'Well, that was a complete waste of time coming here!' he sighed heavily. 'We could have been told all that on the phone!'

'Maybe not,' said a voice behind him.

Jake and Lauren swung round, and came face to face with the girl who'd been arguing with the receptionist.

'What do you mean?' asked Jake.

'Meaning I'm here,' said the girl. 'And if you want to know something about the de Courceys, then I'm your girl.'

Lauren frowned.

'Who are you?' she asked.

'Gemma Hayward,' said the girl. 'My mum used to work for the de Courceys at the hall.'

'And how do you think you can help us?' asked Lauren guardedly.

The girl gave a sly grin.

'Because you're going to have a job trying to find out about that bunch of crooks from anyone else.' She gave a sour face as she jerked her thumb at the door of the solicitors. 'That lot, all the de Courceys' high and mighty friends around here, they all stick together. But me,' her face darkened, 'I know what they're really like. Me and my mum have been on the receiving end.'

'What do you mean?' asked Lauren.

Gemma looked around, suspicious.

'We can't talk here,' she said. 'They might hear us, and the next second they'll have me in court for slander or something, like that cow up there threatened.'

'You *really* know the de Courceys?' asked Jake, still feeling that this was just a wind-up of some sort.

'Know them? Me and my mum lived with 'em!' said Gemma. She gestured along the high street. 'Look, if you want to buy me a coffee, I'll tell you all about 'em.'

'Why would you do that?' asked Jake, puzzled.

'Because if you're asking about them, I reckon they've got something of yours, same way they've got something of ours. And maybe we can work together.'

'Maybe we can.' Lauren nodded. 'So, where's a good place for coffee in this town?'

# Chapter 15

Jake and Lauren followed Gemma down the hill back into the new part of Sevenoaks. As they walked, they passed various coffee shops that looked inviting, but Gemma headed for a burger bar.

'The coffee's rubbish, but the fries are good,' Gemma told them.

Jake left Lauren with Gemma while he went to the counter and ordered three coffees and a portion of fries. The coffee smelt like cheap instant stuff.

He sat the tray down, and Gemma immediately began to tuck into the fries.

'Gemma was telling me that her mum worked as a maid for Guy's dad,' said Lauren.

'Yeah.' Gemma nodded. 'The old earl. Earl Edwyn. The one who died. We had a small cottage on the estate. Anyway, the old earl promised my mum that whatever happened, we'd be all right. He'd look after us.' She scowled as she stuffed more fries into her mouth. 'The next thing we know is he's selling up and we get kicked out without a penny in redundancy money! Now we're living in a caravan park and she's on benefits. After all my mum did for them!'

'They cheated you,' said Jake sympathetically.

'Yeah!' Gemma took a sip of her coffee, and her face creased in distaste. 'Yuck! This stuff's gross, even worse than I remembered it. I should have had a milkshake.'

Lauren shot a meaningful look at Jake, and he asked Gemma, 'Would you like a milkshake?'

'Yeah.' Gemma nodded. 'Vanilla. A large one.'

Jake headed back to the counter and bought a large milkshake. When he returned to the table, Gemma was still venting her tale of being cheated.

'Gemma says she wants to sue the de Courceys,' Lauren told Jake as he sat down.

'The estate owes us!' said Gemma vehemently. 'If I had the money I'd sue them!'

'We haven't got any money,' said Jake quickly. Too quickly, because he felt a sharp kick from Lauren. But either Gemma hadn't heard Jake, or she'd decided to ignore him.

'My mum's soft,' she continued. 'She says to let it go, put it behind us. My brother says the same. They say it's not the de Courceys' fault because the old earl was broke and couldn't afford to pay her, but I say the estate has still got money somewhere!'

'Do you know Guy de Courcey?' asked Lauren.

Gemma's lips curled.

'Him!' she snorted. 'That's where most of the money went! What a waster! All the time I was growing up, he was having parties, everything he wanted. Spend, spend, spend!'

'We heard he left.'

'Ran away, more like,' said Gemma. 'His dad got fed up with having to bail him out all the time, fixing things, paying his bills. I think he was relieved when he said he was going abroad.'

'How long ago was that?' asked Jake.

Gemma thought. 'Umm. I was about thirteen when he left. I'm fifteen now. So, two years ago.'

'And he never came back?'

Gemma shook her head.

'No, thank God.'

'What about the library?' asked Lauren.

'What about it?' asked Gemma.

'The books in it. Were they sold, or did they stay with the house when it went to the National Trust?'

'Why? Are you after one of the books?'

'We're just trying to find out what happened to them,' said Jake.

'Yeah, well, that was a right rip-off,' said Gemma.

'In what way?'

'A tax dodge,' said Gemma. 'The old earl sold most of the really old books, the ones worth some money, but not everything was declared.' She winked. 'Part-cheque, part-cash. Know what I mean? A deal between him and this bookseller bloke.'

'What bookseller bloke?' asked Jake.

Gemma frowned thoughtfully as she tried to bring the name of the bookseller back.

'Jason something. He was a nice old bloke. Big whiskers, but pleasant. Not snobbish like some of the people who used to hang around the old earl.' She shook her head. 'No, not Jason, something weirder. Jasper. That was it. Jasper Brigstocke. I remember because I saw his card. I thought it was an unusual name.'

'Was he local?' asked Jake.

Gemma shook her head.

'No,' she said. 'London. Somewhere in the West End, I think. I just remember his name.'

'Can you remember what he bought?' asked Lauren.

Gemma shook her head.

'Just a load of old books,' she said. 'A van full.' She stopped sucking on the straw of her milkshake and looked inquisitively at Jake and Lauren. 'Anyway, what are you two after from the de Courceys? Do they owe you money?'

'No,' said Jake. 'Like we said, we were curious to know what happened to the books.' He smiled. 'We're interested in old books.'

Gemma gave a scornful laugh.

'Do me a favour!' she said derisively. 'No one comes all this way just to look for some old books.'

'Jasper Brigstocke did,' pointed out Jake.

'Yeah, but that's cos he was gonna make money out of 'em. No one does nothing if there ain't a profit in it. What you *really* after?'

'Just some of the old books!' repeated Jake.

Gemma looked at them suspiciously.

'All right,' she said. 'You don't want to tell me, that's fine. But I can tell that you're after something from the de Courceys. So why don't we work together? I know all about them. I can put you on to stuff. We can all benefit from this.'

'I'm sorry,' said Lauren apologetically. 'It really is just the books we're interested in.'

Gemma sucked on her milkshake for a while longer, still studying them. Then she gave a toss of her head and said airily, 'Well, if that's your story, all right. But if you change your mind, we'd be better off working together on this.'

'What makes you think we can be any help to you with the de Courceys?' asked Lauren.

'For one thing, you're older than me,' said Gemma. 'Like I said, I'm only fifteen. I can't sue people on my

133

own, and my mum don't want to get involved. But you can.'

'Why would we want to sue the de Courceys?'

'That's your business,' said Gemma. 'But, like I say, whatever it is, we'll get better results working together.'

'OK,' said Jake. 'We'll think about it.'

'Where can we get hold of you if we need to?' asked Lauren.

Gemma took out a scrap of paper and wrote an address on it in scrawling letters.

'This is the park where we live,' she said. Beneath the address, she wrote a mobile number. 'And this is my mobile. What about yours?'

Jake was reluctant to give their details to this girl. She seemed intense. She'd already hung around outside in the street and waited for them at the solicitor's office. He was worried that if they gave Gemma their address, she'd turn up at their flat and start harassing them.

Fortunately, Lauren had had the same doubts, and was already handling it. Lauren wrote her mobile number on a torn-off piece of the table napkin, adding her name after it.

'This is my mobile,' she said. 'We're in between places at the moment, so we can't give you an address.'

'Mobile's fine,' said Gemma.

She took out her mobile and dialled the number Lauren had written. Immediately, Lauren's mobile rang.

'That's all right then.' Gemma smiled, clicking her phone off and cutting the call.

A shadow fell over the table and they heard a young man say, 'Gemma!' in a weary tone of voice.

They looked up. A boy of about eighteen was standing there, looking at Gemma, and Jake and Lauren could see at once the family resemblance between them. Her brother, thought Jake.

'What?' demanded Gemma irritably.

'I just had a phone call from Mrs Ward at the solicitor's,' he said. He let out a groan. 'Gemma, you've got to stop doing this!'

'Doing what?' demanded Gemma.

'You know what I mean,' he said. He looked at Jake and Lauren, and then appealed to Gemma: 'Maybe it'd be better if we talked about this outside, in private.'

'No!' said Gemma firmly.

'They're talking about taking out an injunction against you for harassment,' he said.

'Oh yeah!' snapped Gemma. 'I'd like to see 'em try!'

'They're solicitors, Gemma . . .'

'Yeah, small-town solicitors,' sneered Gemma. 'Well, I'm gonna get me some big-time solicitors, and then we'll see what that creep Ainsworth does!'

'Gemma, this is crazy talk . . .'

'Oh yeah? You're just prepared to take it lying down, are you? Just like Mum. Well, I ain't! You can do whatever you want, Dan. Me, I'm going to get what's rightfully mine!'

With that she got to her feet, pushed past him and stormed out of the burger bar. He stood looking after her, helpless.

'Trouble?' asked Lauren sympathetically.

He turned back to them.

'It's not your problem,' he said.

'In a way it is,' said Lauren. 'We're after some information about the de Courcey family.'

The boy gave them a look filled with bitterness and suspicion.

'You're planning to sue them as well, are you?' he demanded.

'No, absolutely not!' Lauren hastened to assure him. 'We were interested in the old library at the hall, that's all. Gemma offered to tell us about it.'

'We met her at the solicitor's,' added Jake. 'We'd gone there to see Mr Ainsworth.'

Dan sighed, and then sank down on to the seat his sister had just left.

'Then you heard the row?' he asked.

'Yes,' said Lauren. 'It was a bit of a shouting match.'

'I don't know what to do about her,' he said, forcing a small smile at them. 'I'm Dan, by the way, Gemma's brother.'

'We guessed that,' said Lauren. 'Family resemblance.'

'Only in looks,' sighed Dan. 'We're pretty different. She's always flying off the handle, losing her temper. Me, I prefer a quiet life. Yeah, I was angry over what had happened with us being kicked out of our cottage and ending up in a caravan, but you can't go on being bitter all your life. It just eats at you. Like it's doing with Gemma.'

'What did Gemma mean when she spoke about getting some *real* lawyers?' asked Jake.

Dan shrugged and let out a heartfelt sigh.

'Yesterday we had a phone call at home from this firm of solicitors in London. Pierce Randall, they called themselves.'

At the mention of the name Jake tensed, and he felt Lauren fidgeting beside him.

'What did they want?' asked Jake, doing his best to make his voice sound casual.

'They wanted to talk about the de Courcey family.' He frowned. 'In fact, it was something about a book.' He looked questioningly at Jake and Lauren. 'Is that why you're here? You mentioned the library at the hall. Are you after the same thing?' Suddenly his questioning look turned into one of suspicion. 'Are you from Pierce Randall?'

'No,' said Lauren. 'I promise.' Swiftly she changed the subject, asking, 'How did Gemma know about them if they phoned *you*?'

'She was listening. She's always does that, eavesdropping. They said there could be money in it for us. She heard me tell them I wasn't interested, and she got angry. She said I was an idiot to turn down the chance of getting what we were owed. I bet that's what she's doing now. Getting on to these Pierce Randall people.' He shook his head. 'No good's going to come of it. I told her, she's only going to get us in trouble, but she won't listen to me.'

# Chapter 16

As Jake and Lauren walked back to Sevenoaks railway station, they talked about Gemma and Pierce Randall.

'Once she tells them about Jasper Brigstocke, they'll be moving in on him,' said Jake. 'We need to get to him first.'

'I still think it's all too simple,' insisted Lauren. 'There's no way we're just going to walk into his book-shop and find The Index on his shelves.'

'There is if he doesn't know what it is,' said Jake. 'Think about it. If it just looks like a book with a list of place names, as far as he's concerned it's nothing more than finding an old phone book. It's nothing special. Not like a first edition of Dickens, or an original Shakespeare.'

'So why would he have bought it in the first place?'

'Because he'd have seen that it's from the fifteenth century, so it's bound to be worth something to some book collector.'

Lauren thought it over and then said, 'Maybe you're right.'

Jake was already checking out Jasper Brigstocke on his iPhone.

'Got him,' he said. 'Jasper Brigstocke, antiquarian books. His shop is in Notting Hill Gate.'

Jake dialled the number. It rang, and then went to voicemail. A man's voice said, 'This is Jasper Brigstocke. I'm afraid I'm not available at the moment, so do leave a message and I will get back to you in due course.'

Jake hung up.

'He's not there,' he said. 'Or, he is, but he's not answering the phone.'

'Then let's hope we get to him before Pierce Randall do,' said Lauren.

Sue Clark sat at her desk, scanning a row of figures on a balance sheet. They were from the accounts of a large multinational company, which the tax authorities were accusing of fraud and tax evasion. Of course it was tax evasion; her job, along with the firm's account- ants, was to prove this was a case of tax avoidance, an entirely different and perfectly legal situation. Her desk phone rang. It was her secretary.

'I've got a Gemma Hayward on the line, Ms Clark,' she said. 'She said you were talking to her brother, Dan, the other day.'

Immediately, Clark was alert.

'Put her through,' she said.

Jasper Brigstocke's Antiquarian Bookshop was a narrow-fronted shop on a tiny old street about halfway between Notting Hill Gate and Queensway underground stations. Although the surrounding area was busy with traffic and people, this street was virtually deserted; just a few people using it as a short cut between the main thoroughfares.

The shop was ancient. The door and window displays were dusty. The books in the window looked as if they'd been there even longer than the shop.

'It doesn't look like a business that makes a lot of money,' commented Jake.

'Maybe that's just a cover,' suggested Lauren. 'Keeps the tax man off his back.'

Jake was about to push the door to go in, when he saw that the sign hanging inside the glass panel said 'Closed'.

'What!' he scowled. 'Closed! We've come all this way for nothing!'

Lauren pressed her nose against the glass. As she did so, the door swung inwards.

Jake and Lauren exchanged puzzled looks.

'D'you think he'd really go out and leave his shop unlocked?' asked Jake. 'Especially in London.'

'Maybe he just forgot to turn the "Closed" sign back to "Open",' suggested Lauren.

She pushed the door open wider and stepped in, Jake close behind her.

The shop had been trashed. Books had been pulled from the shelves and lay scattered on the floor.

'Trouble,' whispered Jake apprehensively.

'Hello!' Lauren called. 'Mr Brigstocke!'

There was no answer.

'Maybe we should call the police,' she muttered.

'Let's see if Brigstocke's here first,' said Jake. 'He may have already done that.'

The shop, although narrow, seemed never-ending. As they walked through it, doing their best to avoid treading on the books on the floor, they could see that it widened out, as if it expanded into the neighbouring shops.

It was a maze of very tall free-standing wooden shelves that formed alleyways. Each shelf must have been stacked with books, most of which were now ankle-deep on the floor.

Again, Lauren called out, 'Mr Brigstocke!' There was no reply, just a silence hanging over the whole shop.

They moved along one of the narrow alleyways, over the carpet of scattered books, and finally, at the back of the shop they came to a door with the word 'Office' on a nameplate fixed to it.

Jake rapped on the door, at the same time calling, 'Mr Brigstocke! Hello!'

There was still no answer.

The door swung inwards.

'Mr Brigstocke?' said Jake, stepping inside. Then he stopped.

'What's the matter?' asked Lauren.

'Don't come in,' said Jake, his voice shaking.

He tried to stop Lauren, but it was too late. Lauren uttered a sound that was half scream, half groan.

A man was tied to a high-backed wooden chair. He was dead; that was obvious from the lifeless eyes staring out from the pale bloodstained face. But what was worse was the sight of the fingers on the floor by his feet, and the dried blood smearing the wooden chair near his hand, where those fingers had once been.

# Chapter 17

Lauren stumbled outside the room and suddenly threw up. Jake knew how she felt; at the sight of Jasper Brigstocke's dead and mutilated body, he could feel the contents of his own stomach rising up in his throat, but he did his best to keep them down.

'We have to call the police,' panted Lauren.

'No,' said Jake. 'Bullen will think we did this, and he'll lock me up. We have to stay free if we're going to prove our innocence.'

Lauren shook her head, her face deathly pale.

'Do you think Pierce Randall did this?' she asked hoarsely.

'I don't know,' said Jake. 'All I know is we have to get out of here, and fast.'

A short time later Jake and Lauren were in a café at Marble Arch; their cups of coffee sat on the table, untouched. For both of them, the image of Jasper Brigstocke, tortured to death, filled their minds.

'We have to get a hold of ourselves,' Jake whispered. 'And we have to move fast. Once the police discover Brigstocke's body and they start checking for finger-prints, they'll find ours at the shop and they'll put out a search for us.'

'How do we stop them?' asked Lauren. She was still in a state of shock.

'Just like we said before: we find The Index,' said Jake. 'It's not just the proof about the Order of Malichea, and why all this has been happening, it's our bargaining tool. Pierce Randall, MI5, everyone will make sure we're free if we've got that.'

'But we haven't!' hissed Lauren. 'And if Brigstocke had it, then it's gone! Whoever killed him will have forced him to tell them where it was in the shop, and they'll have taken it!'

Jake shook his head.

'I don't think Brigstocke had it. If he did, he would have told them. Why hold out under torture like that for a book? The fact they did those dreadful things to him means they weren't getting the answers they wanted. Brigstocke didn't have it.'

'So where is it?' agonised Lauren.

Jake stared into his cup of coffee, at the dark liquid, the touches of froth on the side. Think, he urged himself. Think! The de Courcey family were given The Index for safe keeping after Glastonbury was destroyed. Where would they have put it? In plain sight, in the library? Or would they have hidden it somewhere? The book was precious, very precious. They wouldn't have taken a chance on leaving it in the library for anyone to see.

Suddenly a thought struck him. Something Guy had said when they'd been in the cell at the police station.

He looked at Lauren, his eyes suddenly alive, agitated.

'I think I know what happened to The Index!' he said.

Lauren studied him, a doubtful expression on her face.

'You're sure this isn't just coming out of desperation, Jake?'

'No.' He leant towards her. 'Guy told me his family backed the wrong side in the Civil War, so they supported King Charles I and his cavaliers.'

'Yes.' Lauren nodded. 'So?'

'Well, it's common knowledge that Catholics sided with the cavaliers. And we know that a de Courcey ancestor headed up the Order of Malichea at Glastonbury in the 1500s. So what does this tell us about the de Courcey family?'

Lauren thought about it.

'That the de Courceys were Catholics,' she said.

'And wealthy Catholic families in the time of Henry VIII, certainly later Henry, and when Queen Elizabeth I was on the throne, often kept their religion secret to avoid persecution and having their wealth taken from them,' said Jake.

Lauren stared at Jake, and now her face looked as excited as his.

'And wealthy Catholic families had special hiding places in their houses to keep items of their religion.'

'Not just items,' Jake reminded her. 'They even hid their priests.'

'Priest's holes!' nodded Lauren. 'Hidden chambers.' Then her face clouded over. 'But surely, such a hiding place at de Courcey Hall would have been discovered by now, after all these years.'

'Yes,' agreed Jake. 'And who's likely to know if such a place was discovered, and what happened to the stuff that was in it?'

'You're thinking Gemma and Dan Hayward?' queried Lauren.

Jake nodded. 'I am.'

Lauren frowned.

'It's a long shot,' she said.

'Everything about this business has always been a long shot,' said Jake.

'And if The Index had turned up, Gemma and Dan would have seen it. Especially Gemma. She's got a real nose for finding things out.'

'Yes, but she wouldn't know what The Index was. We do! We know what we're looking for!' said Jake. 'We have to talk to Gemma!'

# Chapter 18

Jake checked his watch as they left the café.

'Half past six,' he said.

'We can't go back to our flat,' said Lauren. 'If the police have found Brigstocke's body and put out a search for us, that'll be the first place they'll look.'

'I suggest we head back to Sevenoaks,' agreed Jake. 'We'll go and see Gemma and see what she can tell us, if anything. Then we'll stay at a hotel near there for the night.'

'And the priest's hole?'

'We'll go to de Courcey Hall first thing tomorrow morning and start looking for it.'

'That won't be easy. It's National Trust, remember. They're not going to let us start poking around.'

'They might if Gemma's able to give us some information about where it might be, and the Trust don't know about it.'

Lauren looked doubtful.

'There's a lot of *ifs* there,' she pointed out. '*If* there is a priest's hole. *If* Gemma tells us where it is. *If* the National Trust let us look for it.'

'You got any better suggestions?'

'No,' she admitted.


Jake and Lauren arrived at the caravan park on the edge of Sevenoaks at eight. They followed the driveways until they came to South Avenue, and number 36. They rang the bell and Dan Hayward opened the door.

'Hi,' he said. 'I didn't expect to see you two.'

'We didn't expect to be back here,' said Jake. 'Is Gemma in?'

Dan shook his head, and they could see he was worried.

'Soon after you left, I had a text from her to say she was going to London to see that firm of lawyers I told you about, Pierce Randall.'

'She actually went to see them?'

Dan nodded. 'Then she texted me again about six to say she'd just seen a lawyer there called Sue Clark, and she was staying up in London overnight and not to worry.'

'But you haven't spoken to her?'

'No, just texts. I tried phoning her, but I keep getting her voicemail.' He looked at them, concern written all over his face. 'What's she up to?'

'Doing what she said she would, by the sound of it: getting hold of a hotshot lawyer to sue the de Courceys.'

'Which she could find difficult,' added Lauren. 'Pierce Randall are also Guy de Courcey's solicitors.'

Dan looked even more worried.

'I don't get any of this,' he said.

'I think we ought to tell him what's going on,' Lauren said to Jake. 'If Gemma's got herself involved with Pierce Randall, he has a right to know what's behind it.'

'What do you mean?' asked Dan, a new note of urgency in his voice. 'What's going on? Is it dangerous?'

'Can we come in and talk?' Lauren asked.

Dan nodded.

'Sure. Mum's out seeing a friend of hers,' he said. 'There's just me here.'

'Good,' said Lauren.

Inside, the trailer was big and comfortable. Jake was aware that it looked larger and a lot tidier than his and Lauren's flat.

Dan offered them coffee, and while he made it, Jake and Lauren took turns to fill him in on the situation they found themselves in: starting right back with the ancient Order of Malichea, the hidden library, and the shooting of Alex Munro, and Jake and Guy finding themselves in a police cell. They didn't tell him about finding Jasper Brigstocke's mutilated body, deciding that would only send him into a panic about Gemma's safety.

They finished by telling him that the book everyone, including them, was looking for was The Index, the list of where all the secret books were hidden.

'And Guy's involved?' asked Dan.

Jake and Lauren nodded.

Dan put their coffees down on the table for them, looking thoughtful.

'He was a bad one, Guy,' he said.

'That's what your sister said.'

'She's right. And you think he's been abducted? Taken prisoner?'

'We know he has,' said Lauren. 'Like we said, we saw him at de Courcey Hall, being put into an SUV at gunpoint.'

Dan took out his mobile and dialled.

'This is starting to sound too dangerous,' he told them. 'I'm calling Gemma again.'

They all listened as they heard the ringing tone, then the automated voice cutting in telling Dan to leave a message.

'Hi, Gemma,' said Dan. 'It's Dan. Call me. It's urgent.'

He hung up and turned back to Jake and Lauren.

'So, what's the next move?' he asked.

'If we can get our hands on The Index we think it'll solve this business once and for all. Everyone will stop looking for it.'

'And you think the de Courceys have it?'

'*Had* it,' corrected Lauren. 'And we also think they hid it somewhere.'

'Do you know of any hiding places in the hall?' asked Jake. 'You know, a priest's hole, or somewhere they used to hide religious things?'

Dan thought about it, his brow furrowed.

'Not that I can think of,' he said. 'Everywhere at the hall was opened up just before the old earl handed it over to the National Trust. There were no hidden rooms, no priest's holes or anything like that.'

Jake felt a crushing sense of disappointment descend on him, like a dead weight. In that one sentence, all his hopes of finding The Index had been destroyed.

'Mind, there was Platt Castle,' said Dan thoughtfully.

Jake and Lauren looked questioningly at Dan.

'Platt Castle?' asked Lauren.

Dan nodded.

'It was the de Courcey's family home before they built de Courcey Hall. It wasn't very big, not how you usually think of a castle.'

'Where was it?'

'The site is only about two miles away from de Courcey Hall. The de Courceys owned all that land around there. The place is derelict now, just a load of broken walls, but there used to be a small chapel in it at one time.'

'Do you know when it was abandoned and why exactly?' asked Jake.

'There's something about it in one of the visitor guidebooks to de Courcey Hall,' said Dan. He got up and went to a bookshelf. 'Mum was given one by the old earl.' He gave a bitter laugh. 'Gemma said it was the only thing Mum ever got from the de Courcey family.'

He opened a slim glossy paperback guide, and flicked through the opening pages, before stopping.

'Here it is,' he said. Aloud, he read: '*The original family home of the de Courceys, Platt Castle, was abandoned during the time of Elizabeth I. It is thought that this was to show their good faith to King Henry VIII, so that he wouldn't accuse them of treason and take their family fortune, which was common practice with Catholic families at the time.*'

'So at the time the abbey at Glastonbury was ransacked when Henry VIII was on the throne and the books from the Order of Malichea given to the de Courcey family, the castle and chapel were still intact and functioning. They didn't abandon them until years after,' said Lauren.

'Which means it's possible that The Index and the *Journal* could have been hidden in a secret place inside the chapel at Platt Castle,' added Jake.

Dan shrugged.

'It's possible,' he said. 'But how do we find out?'

'We go there,' said Jake. 'You said it wasn't far away.'

'Isn't it a bit late to go exploring?' asked Lauren. 'It'll be dark soon.'

'It won't be dark for another hour,' Jake said. 'At least we can go and look at the place.'

'Will it help Gemma stay safe?' asked Dan.

'Possibly,' said Jake.

'OK,' said Dan. 'I'll go and get my bike.'

'A bike?' asked Lauren. 'How do *we* get there?'

'It's a motorbike,' clarified Dan. 'And it's got a side-car. We use it for getting the shopping. Cheaper than running a car.'

As Dan left the trailer to go and get his motorbike, Jake turned to Lauren and said, 'You heard what Dan said about Gemma seeing Sue Clark?'

Lauren nodded.

'It was about half past four when we found Jasper Brigstocke's dead body in his shop,' she said, shuddering at the memory of it. 'If Gemma didn't tell Sue Clark about Jasper Brigstocke until just before six, then it couldn't have been Pierce Randall who tortured and killed him.'

'Unless they'd already found out about the sale of the books some other way.'

'Possibly, though I'm starting to think that someone else killed him,' said Lauren.

'The Mexicans?' suggested Jake. 'They had knives.'

'Who knows,' said Lauren. 'We've seen before with these books, there's nearly always someone else in the picture that we don't know about.' She looked nervous as she added, 'I think there's someone else at work here, someone *really* nasty, and we don't know who they are.'

'Think they're watching us?' asked Jake.

'I don't know,' admitted Lauren. 'I hope not. Because, if they are, we're in more danger than we think we are.'

# Chapter 19

Dan pulled up the bike in front of a wooden gate set in a high wire fence. The gate marked a gap in a thickly wooded area, but the track from the gate curved and twisted among the trees, so it was impossible to get a real view of what lay behind the fence.

The gate was closed and looked ramshackle, like it hadn't been opened for many years. Beside it was a battered sign that said: 'Platt Castle. Private property. No entry.'

'This is it,' said Dan. 'We walk from here.'

As they took off their crash helmets and put them in the sidecar, Dan said, worried, 'I still haven't heard from Gemma.'

'I'm sure she's OK,' said Lauren. 'She seems a very resourceful girl.'

'She is,' agreed Dan, but he didn't seem reassured. 'Anyway, I texted her to tell her we were coming here, just in case she gets home and wonders where I am.'

Jake and Lauren followed Dan as he climbed over the gate. They made their way along the rough winding track, through a jungle of trees, until they turned a final bend and saw a clearing ahead, and at the far side of the clearing, the outline of the castle.

Castle was too grand a name for it; the building was more the size of an old manor house. Although, when the place had been built, many hundreds of years ago, it would have been an imposing building. It had thick stone walls; but the tops, where battlements would once have been, were long gone.

They followed Dan to an area at one side of the derelict building.

'This is the site of the old chapel,' said Dan.

It was a small area, not much bigger than a large room in a house. All that was left were the flagstones of the floor and the remains of the stone walls. Ivy and weeds had grown up over and through all that was left of the walls. Rubble, broken stones and more weeds were spread across the floor.

'Where do we start?' asked Lauren.

'We tap the floor,' said Jake. 'Listening for where it sounds hollow.'

Lauren looked doubtful.

'Come on,' encouraged Jake. 'Let's start by

tapping all over, and see if there's any difference in the sound.'

With that, Jake picked up a piece of broken rusted metal from the debris lying around, and began to knock it on the flagstones. Lauren copied him, but Jake stopped her.

'I think we can only do this with one of us,' he said. 'It makes it hard to hear if we're all knocking at the same time.'

'OK,' said Lauren. 'We'll do the listening while you tap.'

Jake resumed tapping the piece of metal against the flagstones, moving from one flagstone to another. Each time they heard the same dull solid thud.

'The light's going,' said Dan. 'We might have to come back tomorrow.'

'Just a bit longer,' urged Jake.

He banged the piece of metal down on the next flag stone. Once again, there was the same dull thud.

'I don't think we're going to find it,' said Lauren gloomily. 'Jake, admit it, this was always going to be a bit of a crazy idea.'

Jake didn't reply. He moved on to the next flagstone. Once more, there was that same dull solid sound. He moved on to the next and banged the metal bar again . . . and this time he stopped.

'There!' he said. 'Did you hear that?'

'What?' asked Lauren.

'It sounded different,' said Jake. 'Listen.'

And he banged the piece of metal on the flagstone again.

Dan frowned.

'Actually, it *did* sound a bit different,' he said.

Using the metal bar, Jake scraped away the dirt around the four edges of the flagstone, and he pushed it in, trying to get leverage. After a bit of pushing and manipulating, the end of the bar was in the crack. Jake pressed down on the end of the bar but the flagstone didn't budge.

'Let me help,' said Dan.

Dan and Jake put all their strength into forcing the bar downwards and slowly that edge of the flagstone began to lift.

'Right,' said Jake. 'See if you can lift it up while I hold the bar in place.'

Dan and Lauren joined Jake, putting their fingers under the edges of the flagstone, and hauling back. It began to lift . . . then Dan and Lauren slid it to one side. There was a hole in the ground beneath where the stone had been, and inside the hole was an object wrapped in oiled black leather.

With trembling fingers, Jake lifted the object out. It felt like a book. Was it The Index? There was only one way to find out. He began to untie the oiled twine that held the package together.

'Do you think that's a good idea?' asked Lauren nervously. 'Some of the books can be booby-trapped. Remember the toxic bacteria inside the first book that was found!'

'If it was hidden here at the chapel, I don't think it would be one of the Malichea science books,' said Jake. 'I'm pretty sure this is one of the books that the abbot gave to the de Courcey family, the *Journal of the Order of Malichea* or The Index.'

'And if you're wrong?' asked Lauren.

Jake didn't reply, but silently he hoped that he was right.

He undid the last piece of twine and peeled back the protective leather covering. Inside was a book, with the familiar symbol of the Order of Malichea inscribed on the cover. He opened it up and saw the ornate Latin writing on the first page, and then continuing on the other pages, each section in a different handwriting, and dated.

'It's the *Journal*,' said Jake, and this excitement at having finally found it was mixed with bitter disappointment that it wasn't the book he'd been hoping to find. 'So where is The Index?' he groaned.

'My question exactly,' said a voice behind them.

# Chapter 20

They swung round, and were shocked to see Guy standing with two young teenage boys, one of whom they'd seen holding a gun on Guy in the car park at de Courcey Hall. Now, the gun was in Guy's hand.

'Don't try anything, any of you,' warned Guy. 'This is a Hechler and Koch MP5K. Very powerful, and with a 30-round clip. Right now it's on automatic, so it'll cut you all in half before you've got within an inch of me.' He smiled. 'I know a lot about guns. They're a sort of hobby of mine.' His smile broadened. 'Dan! Well, well! My old boyhood pal!'

Jake shot a look at Dan, and saw from the grim and sickly look on his face that whatever Guy and Dan had been during their childhood at de Courcey Hall, they hadn't been mates. Dan looked frightened.

Jake turned back to Guy.

'I thought you were in trouble,' Jake said accusingly. 'Being held prisoner.'

'Yes, that's what you were supposed to think,' said Guy. He looked up at the sky. 'It really is starting to get dark. I think we ought to continue this inside.' He jerked the gun. 'Follow Spider. I'll be bringing up the rear. And, like I said, any funny business . . . You're dead.'

Spider led the way towards the ruin of Platt Castle. Jake, Lauren and Dan followed anxiously, aware of Guy and the second boy behind them.

'Make sure you don't drop that book, Jake,' said Guy.

Jake could see that there were glimmers of light coming from the ruined castle. One corner of the interior had survived; it looked as if it had been repaired in a rough sort of fashion. The dim light was showing through a narrow gap where a wooden shutter had been put into place over a small window.

Spider reached a door, opened it, and disappeared inside. Jake, Lauren and Dan followed him, uncomfortably aware of the gun in Guy's hand behind them.

The room was lit by oil lamps and had been kitted out with tatty-looking tables and chairs. Four young people were sprawled on the floor, sitting and lying on sleeping bags. They stood up as Spider led everyone in, their eyes watchful when they saw Jake, Lauren and Dan.

These four also seemed little more than kids. They looked like clones of each other with their sharp-eyes and rat-like faces. Feral. Dangerous.

'Take their mobiles off them, Spider,' Guy said. 'And, you, put your hands above your heads and remember what I said. Try anything and I'll shoot you.'

'What's this about, Guy?' demanded Jake, as Spider began to rummage through their pockets.

'What it's always been about, Jake. Finding The Index,' said Guy. 'Looks like you've got the closest so far. Brownie points to Jake. Or was it your girlfriend who worked it out? You did say she knew more about this business than you did.'

'I got their mobiles, Guy,' said Spider, holding them up. 'You want me to trash them?'

'Yes, but take out the SIM cards and break them first.' Guy looked at Jake and Lauren. 'Just making sure we can't be tracked here. No signals any more; I want to make sure we're safe from interruptions. First, allow me to introduce my friends. Or, my crew, as we like to call ourselves.' He pointed at the boy who'd taken their phones and was busy destroying them. They now saw that he had a tattoo of a spider on his neck. 'Spider, you've met.'

He pointed at the other boy who'd been with him and Spider outside. 'That's Patch. Say hello to Patch, Jake.'

Jake looked at the boy. He looked about fifteen. Like Spider, Patch had a shaved head and a cold, hard stare. He also had what appeared to be a birthmark under his left eye.

'Seems like Jake doesn't want to talk to you at the moment, Patch,' said Guy. 'Don't worry, he will.'

At the threat in Guy's words, Jake felt a sickness in his stomach. We are in big, *big* trouble.

Guy's arm swung round, pointing at two girls. They looked about thirteen, although — with their shapeless clothes and their almost shaven heads — it was difficult to tell.

'Gadge and Midge,' said Guy. 'They are *so* clever, both of them. They can do things with a computer that will amaze you. Manipulation. Getting through encryptions.' He looked at them admiringly. 'I don't know where they could have learnt such skills, but they have been absolutely invaluable to me!'

The two girls beamed broadly at this flattery, smiling at one another, and then looking at Guy with unconcealed admiration.

He's charmed them, realised Jake. He's charmed them all. That's what Guy does.

'Next to Gadge and Midge, that tall guy is Des, my muscleman.'

Jake noticed that Des, who was perhaps a year older than the other kids, wore heavy, metal rings on the fingers of his right hand, which made his fist a formidable weapon.

'Next to Des, that's Patch's brother, Duke.'

Duke, skinheaded like his brother and wearing a street sports outfit, looked to be not much older than fourteen. He had picked up a wicked-looking machete which he flexed as he gave Jake and the others a cruel smile.

At the sight of the weapon, Jake thought of Jasper Brigstocke, his fingers cut off and lying on the floor beside his dead body.

'So that's my crew.' Guy smiled. 'Crew, meet Jake Wells and his girlfriend, Lauren. They're the ones who are going to make us all very rich. The other one with them is Dan, an old boyhood friend of mine.' And Guy laughed at that, a nasty laugh.

Another realisation hit Jake, making him feel very sick. *The fact he's told us the names of his crew, and let us see their faces, means we're not going to get out of here alive.*

'The book, Jake,' said Guy, holding out his hand.

Jake held out the *Journal*, and Guy walked over and took it. He smiled.

'A pity it's not The Index, but it shows you're on the right track, which is good.' He chuckled. 'Just think, all this time it was right here, and I never realised. Do you think The Index is buried out there as well, Jake?'

'Perhaps,' said Jake.

'Well, we'll find out tomorrow,' said Guy. 'It's too dark to start looking now. So, for the moment, we're going to have to put you into storage for the night.'

'Storage?' queried Jake.

166

Guy gestured at the floor.

'The dungeons. The one part of this that's still intact. What do you think of the place, by the way? It's really quite cosy. The old man had it patched up a few years ago. I think he was thinking of opening it as a visitor attraction, to try and bring in some money.' He looked around at the stone walls, eerie in the flickering light from the oil lamps. 'Of course the builders were a bunch of cowboys. But then, my old man was never much of a judge of character. He always seemed to employ useless people.' He gave Dan a nasty smile. 'Like your mother. She got kicked out in the end, though.'

Jake saw Dan tense, and his fists clench at this insult, but he kept mute.

He knows how dangerous Guy is, Jake realised. He knows that Guy is goading him, hoping to provoke an outburst, to give him an excuse to have his crew attack Dan.

Guy said, 'I used to spend time here when I was a kid. It was my hidey-hole. My secret camp. I brought Dan here a couple of times. Do you remember that, Dan?'

Dan didn't reply. Bad memories, realised Jake. Very bad memories.

When Dan didn't say anything, Guy obviously lost interest in the game he was playing with him. He turned to his crew and said, 'OK, Des and Duke, take them down to the dungeons.'

As the two boys moved towards them, Guy added, 'I wouldn't try anything. They will hurt you very badly if you do.'

Des went first, then Jake, Lauren and Dan, with Duke and his machete bringing up the rear. As they walked down some uneven stone steps, the light from Duke's torch lit up the blackness of the ancient dungeons below. The sweet decaying smell of damp earth hit Jake's nostrils. In the torchlight he saw a door made of iron bars. It looked to be hundreds of years old, but the padlock and chain on it were new. Des unlocked it, and opened the door. Jake, Lauren and Dan walked in hesitantly. Des pulled the iron-barred door closed, and snapped the padlock on it shut.

'Call out and Duke here will come down and cut you,' threatened Des.

Then the two headed back up the stairs, the vanishing light of their torch plunging the dungeon into darkness.

Jake's eyes became accustomed to the gloom. Moonlight came in from a tiny hole high up in the wall, over which wire mesh had been fixed, giving him enough light to be able to make out more of the cell.

There was a rustling sound from the deep shadows in the far corner of the room. What was it? Rats? No, it was something much larger, a shape moving in the darkness.

'Hello!' called out Jake nervously.

The rustling stopped, and a voice said, 'Jake? Lauren? Is that you?'

Even though the voice was weak and thin, Jake recognised it.

'Gareth!'

He hurried over to the figure lying on the ground, and recoiled at the sight. Gareth's face was a mess. Even in this gloom, Jake could see dried blood was streaked across it.

'My God, Gareth!' he burst out. 'What have they done to you?'

'It's not as bad as it looks,' said Gareth. 'They just roughed me up a bit. Nothing broken. No serious damage.'

'I phoned your home,' said Lauren. 'Your wife didn't know where you were.'

'No one does, or I'd have been out of here by now,' said Gareth bitterly.

'How is that possible?' asked Jake, astonished. 'MI5 are supposed to know everything! How come they haven't traced you?'

'Because our info mainly covers terrorists, known criminal organisations and the like. What you might term "the usual suspects". MI5 would have been concentrating their efforts to find me on all of them. Unfortunately, a rogue individual like Guy de Courcey is generally well under the radar.

'So what happened?' asked Jake. 'How did you get here?'

'Guy de Courcey contacted me and told me he had some of the Malichea books for sale,' said Gareth. 'He said he'd been told by Pierce Randall they were worth a lot of money, so he was offering them to the highest bidder. He wanted to meet me to see what I'd bid. He said because of his "precarious position" with Pierce Randall, he couldn't afford to meet with me openly, so he asked me to meet him at a secret rendezvous, and to come alone.' He gave a harsh and bitter laugh. 'For possibly the first time in my life, I believed it would be that simple. Or, at least, I felt sure that I was capable of dealing with the situation.

'He started to ask me where The Index was. I use the word "ask" but he was pretty violent. I told him I didn't know, but, of course, he didn't believe me. Then, after days of him getting no leads, he dumped me down here.' In the gathering darkness they saw him shake his head. 'I think he's insane.'

'Yes,' said Dan unhappily. 'That about sums up Guy.'

'This is Dan Hayward,' introduced Jake. 'He and his mother and sister used to live on the de Courcey estate before it was given to the National Trust. Dan knew about the old castle, and the site of the old chapel. Dan, this is my boss from work, Gareth Findlay-Weston.'

'So you knew Guy de Courcey when he was a child?' said Gareth.

'Unfortunately,' said Dan bitterly. 'I did my best to keep out of his way. He was three years older than me, used to take pleasure in bullying me. He's cruel. Vicious. He liked hurting people for fun.'

'And he looks like he's found a gang of like-minded bullies,' said Lauren.

'The street crew.' Gareth nodded. 'Yes, he's very proud of them. He took pleasure in telling me how he'd found them.'

'Found them?' queried Jake.

'They were all living together in a squat at the back of King's Cross. Runaways, orphans.' He shook his head. 'OK, they seem dangerous, and a couple of them certainly are, but I don't think they had a chance. If there ever was a safety net for kids like these, they fell well and truly through it.

'Guy stepped in and offered them a way out. And not just a way out, he offered them affection.'

'Affection?' said Dan sarcastically. 'He's a vicious bully!'

'He also knows how to manipulate people,' said Gareth. 'I've seen him at work with these kids. He handles them with a mixture of fear and warmth. And the bottom line is he's offered them a permanent home here, and lots of riches.' He sighed. 'Affection. Money. Security. It's a winning combination.'

'I don't understand it,' said Jake, bewildered. 'When I first met Guy he'd only just arrived in England from Mexico. He wouldn't have had time to set all this up!'

'I'm afraid to disillusion you, Jake, but your friend Guy is a liar.'

'Always was,' put in Dan miserably.

'Just because he told you something it doesn't mean it's true,' continued Gareth. 'As far as I can gather, Guy was back in England some time before he killed Alex Munro, putting together his plan.'

'Guy killed Munro?' echoed Jake, stunned.

Gareth nodded.

'I'm sure he'll tell you all about it,' he said. 'Guy likes to boast about how clever he is. But how did you get here?'

'Like we said, Dan knew about the site of the old chapel,' said Jake.

'Jake worked out that if The Index and the *Journal* had been hidden anywhere, then the old chapel was the most likely place,' added Lauren.

'Impressive!' said Gareth. 'And did you find anything?'

'We found the *Journal* in a hiding place under one of the flagstones,' said Jake. 'We didn't have time to look any more, because Guy turned up at that point, with a gun.'

'Yes, our friend Guy has a fondness for guns,' murmured Gareth. 'And I gather he is quite a good shot. He must be, to have killed Munro the way he did.'

'Why did he kill Munro?' asked Lauren.

'I'm still not sure. He said something about it being part of his plan. I feel that Guy has delusions of grandeur about being some master criminal. And he has no compassion, which makes him a very dangerous person.'

'He's always been a dangerous person,' muttered Dan. 'I think the old earl was glad when he left the country. In fact, I think he was actually frightened of him. I know everyone else was.'

'If he was so dangerous, why didn't anyone spot it before and do something about it?' asked Lauren. 'Like, at school.'

'He's clever,' said Dan. 'And he can be very convincing.'

'That's true,' sighed Jake ruefully. 'He had me convinced.' He fell silent, then said, 'I wonder what he plans to do with us next?'

# Chapter 21

For the next few hours nothing happened. They sat on the damp earth floor in the cell and listened to sounds happening upstairs, but they couldn't hear any voices, just the odd banging noise, or footsteps.

'We'll be OK,' said Dan. 'Remember, I texted Gemma to tell her where we'd gone. If she goes home and finds I'm not there, she'll come looking for me here, and when she sees my motorbike parked, she'll know I'm here.'

'And she'll walk straight into Guy and his gang,' pointed out Jake unhappily.

At that thought, Dan looked even more miserable.

'Don't worry,' Lauren tried to reassure him. 'You said she told you she was staying in London, so she won't be coming here.'

'But say she changes her mind?' asked Dan, very worried.

No one answered him. Jake didn't like to think what would happen to her if she did show up.

About midnight they heard footsteps. It was one of the girls, Gadge. She pushed something through the bars of the cell door.

'Here,' she said.

Then she went back upstairs.

Jake picked up two bottles of water.

'At least we won't die of thirst,' said Lauren.

'When do we get fed?' Jake asked Gareth.

'When they feel like it,' said Gareth. 'I've been here for four days now and have had a few pieces of bread.'

'Why do you think they haven't killed you?' asked Jake.

'I think Guy sees me as a bargaining chip if things go bad for him,' said Gareth. 'From what I can make out, Alex Munro told him about my real job.'

'Your real job?' queried Dan.

'As everyone else here seems to know, I don't see why you should be kept out of the loop,' said Gareth. 'I work for the secret services.' He gave a wry smile. 'But that's a secret, and I expect you to keep it.'

'I will!' Dan assured him.

'Providing we get out of here,' sighed Lauren.

Deep night came. Lauren, Gareth and Dan eventually succumbed to sleep, but Jake stayed awake. Every nerve in his body was twitching. The whole time he was waiting for the sound of footsteps on the stairs and someone to appear with that machete, or Guy with the gun. They're going to kill us, he said to himself. The question is: when? Will Guy keep us as a bargaining chip, the way he's hanging on to Gareth? Unlikely. Gareth's worth something, he's valuable. Me, Lauren and Dan, we're disposable.

By the time daylight filtered in through the tiny hole, Jake still hadn't slept. Lauren, Dan and Gareth woke, and they all took sips from the bottles of water. No one spoke, there wasn't much to say. Nothing positive, anyway.

They sat on the floor, or paced to stretch their legs, as the hours passed. No one came down to the dungeons to see them. One hour passed, then two, then three. They thought they heard sounds of banging and crashing going on somewhere outside, but the sounds were distant.

Finally, at half past eleven, they heard the sound of boots on the stone steps. Duke and Des appeared. As before, Duke was holding the machete.

Des unlocked the door and pointed at Jake and Lauren.

'You two,' he snapped. 'Guy wants to see you.'

Guy was sitting waiting for them as Jake and Lauren were pushed into the room. The other members of the

176

gang were lounging about. From the sullen expressions on their faces and the dirt on their clothes, Jake guessed they'd been digging for The Index at the site of the old chapel. Guy's opening words confirmed this.

'Well, you have kept us busy, Jake,' he said. 'After you found the *Journal*, it really got us quite excited, so we've spent the whole morning, ever since the sun came up, lifting those very heavy flagstones and searching the whole site. And guess what?'

Jake didn't need to guess. The venomous looks he was receiving from the members of Guy's crew said it plainly.

'That's right, Jake. A couple more empty holes, but no sign of The Index. Which is very disappointing. So, Jake, where is it?'

'I don't know,' said Jake.

'Let me have a go at him,' snarled Des. 'I'll make him talk.'

'Wait, Des. Don't be so impatient. I'm sure Jake will be helpful to us, without our having to resort to too much violence.'

Jake looked at the kids' faces. Not all of them would enjoy inflicting pain. Yes, Des and Duke would be nasty, he could tell that. But there was hope in the others: in the two girls, Midge and Gadge. They were part of this crew, but at the same time he had the feeling they were separate from it. The two unknowns were Patch and Spider. Were they cruel, enjoying torture, like Des and Duke? Or did they have something that could be appealed to, deep down?

Guy was talking again.

'You see, Jake, so far out of all the people I've talked to about The Index, or any of the Malichea books, you're the only one who's shown the kind of brains to work out where they are. Munro told me you'd found some of the books. Pierce Randall told me the same. And here you are, successfully tracking down the *Journal*, something that no one has done before. So you see, Jake, I feel you have the power.'

'The power?'

Guy nodded.

'Something inside your brain works things out and comes to the right answer. Where do you *think* it is, Jake?'

'I told you, I don't know!' said Jake firmly.

Guy sighed.

'That's a pity.' He gestured to Patch and Midge. 'Put her in the chair and tie her to it.'

'What?' demanded Jake, shocked.

As Patch grabbed hold of Lauren, Jake saw Midge hesitate.

'Midge!' barked Guy, his tone commanding, and the girl took Lauren's other arm and the two began to drag her towards a heavy wooden armchair.

Jake shouted, 'No!' and leapt at them. There was a flash of metal and he felt a sickening crunch on the side of his head that knocked him to the floor.

He struggled to his hands and knees, dazed, his head hurting, the taste of blood in his mouth.

Duke was grinning nastily down at him, holding the machete.

'He only used the handle that time, Jake,' said Guy. 'Next time it'll be the blade.' He turned to the watching kids and ordered, 'Spider. Des. Take hold of Jake and keep him under control.' To Jake, he added, 'If you do try anything, Jake, it'll be your girlfriend who gets it. Duke here will take a slice out of her.'

'I won't try anything,' Jake promised fervently.

'Good,' said Guy, adding with a mock apologetic tone, 'and, because I can't bear to hear someone scream . . . Gadge, stick some tape over her mouth.'

Gadge came forward, holding a roll of duct tape in her hand. She held out the roll to Duke, and he cut off a length with his machete. Gadge stuck the thick tape over Lauren's mouth, while Midge and Patch continued tying her to the chair.

'Good,' said Guy. 'Duke. Let me have the blade.'

Duke hesitated.

'The blade, Duke!' snapped Guy, and there was no mistaking the authority in his voice.

Sullenly, Duke handed over the machete to Guy. He turned towards Jake, who now had Spider and Des standing very close on either side of him.

'This is the way it's going to be, Jake,' said Guy. 'I ask you a question. If I'm happy with the answer, we can all leave. If I'm not . . .' He brandished the machete. 'Your girlfriend loses a finger. You'll have ten opportunities to tell me what I need to know. After that, I start cutting off other parts of her.'

Once again, the image of Jasper Brigstocke's mutilated body filled Jake's mind.

'No!' pleaded Jake. 'Please, don't hurt her.'

'Give me a reason not to,' said Guy calmly.

He's mad, thought Jake, just as Gareth said. Absolutely insane. There's no way of appealing to him.

'You're not talking, Jake,' said Guy with a sigh. 'You're not telling me what I want to know.' To Patch he said, 'Stretch out her right hand.' To Jake, he said, 'I think we'll start with the little finger. Midge, hold her tightly.'

Again, Midge hesitated, and Jake could see the reluctance on her face. He looked across at Gadge, and saw that she was also very unhappy about what was happening.

But both girls are in too deep, Jake realised. They wouldn't betray Guy.

Midge tightened her grip on Lauren, while Patch took hold of Lauren's right hand and forced her clenched fist open, separating her fingers. Guy raised the machete. Lauren struggled wildly, and Jake could tell she was trying to scream, but the thick tape over her mouth stifled her cries.

'This will hurt,' Guy told her.

'No!' screamed Jake. 'OK, I'll tell you!'

Guy hesitated, the machete still raised.

'As easily as that?' he queried, with a sardonic smile. 'I think you're trying to fool me, Jake, just to stop your girlfriend getting carved up.'

'No,' said Jake desperately. 'I think I know where The Index is.'

There was a pause, and then Guy slowly lowered the weapon.

'If you're lying to me I'll cut off all her fingers and her toes,' he threatened.

'I'm not lying,' said Jake desperately. 'And it's just a guess, but it's the same sort of guess that got me here to find the *Journal*.'

Guy walked over to Jake and stood studying him thoughtfully, the machete still poised in his hands.

'Where is it?'

'I think it's at the place they call the British Area 51. It's a Government base at Laker Heath.'

Guy frowned, trying to work out if Jake was really telling the truth, or if it was just a ploy to save Lauren.

'What makes you think that?' he asked.

'Because the only other place it could have been was here, at the site of the old chapel,' said Jake. 'You said yourself, you found hollow places beneath some of the flagstones you lifted, and I'm guessing they were just like the one where we found the *Journal*.'

Guy's eyes watched Jake. They're like a snake's, thought Jake: he's waiting to strike, but holding off for the moment.

'Go on,' said Guy.

'So my guess is The Index was buried here, but found. We know that it's not Pierce Randall who found it, otherwise they wouldn't still be looking for it. So that leaves the British security services, MI5.'

'But your friend, Mr Findlay-Weston, didn't offer that information when I first asked him,' said Guy suspiciously.

'Maybe he doesn't know it's there,' said Jake desperately. 'It could have been found before his time.'

Guy still looked suspicious.

'Let's say that MI5 had found it,' he said. 'What makes you think it's at this Laker Heath place?'

'Because that's where they keep the stuff they count as weird. Oddball.'

'Flying saucers?' came Des's jeering voice behind Jake's back.

'Yes,' said Jake, keeping his eyes on Guy. 'There's an aircraft hangar on the site where they keep all those sorts of things.'

Guy wasn't laughing, he was thinking.

'If this is a scam to play for time, Jake, I will be very unhappy,' he said. And he brandished the machete. 'I will kill your girlfriend first, right in front of your eyes, very slowly and bit by bit. And then I'll kill you.'

'It's no scam,' said Jake desperately. 'I'm sure that's where The Index is. It's the only place it can be.'

Guy fell silent and began to pace around the room, in deep thought, watched the whole time by Jake and Lauren, and by his crew. Finally, he turned to Patch and Des.

'Bring up Mr Findlay-Weston,' he said. 'I think he and I need to have another conversation.'

# Chapter 22

This time, Gareth was the centre of attention. He'd been forced down to the floor by Patch and Des and sat, looking warily at Guy, who paced around him, the machete swinging casually in his hand. Now, in daylight, Jake could see how badly Gareth had been treated: his face was puffed up and bruised.

Lauren was still tied to the chair, her mouth taped up. Jake was sitting on a rickety wooden chair.

'So, Gareth . . .' said Guy. Then he smiled. 'You don't mind if I call you Gareth, do you? Mr Findlay-Weston seems so formal, and we have known one another intimately for a few days now.'

Gareth shrugged.

'Laker Heath,' said Guy. 'Jake tells me the hangar there is where top-secret things are held.'

Gareth shot a frown of disapproval at Jake.

'So?' he said.

'Is it?' asked Guy.

Gareth didn't reply.

'Slash him!' called Duke.

'Patience, Duke,' said Guy soothingly. To Gareth, he said, 'I will be doing an internet check on the place, see what gossip there is about it. So, ask yourself, in view of that, is it worth dying for?'

'Yes, it does contain top-secret and classified artefacts.'

'Flying saucers?' asked Gadge, and Jake could hear her genuine interest.

'Perhaps,' said Gareth. 'I have never been inside it myself.'

'Oh, come on, Gareth!' scoffed Guy. 'A head of section of MI5!'

'That's why,' said Gareth. 'I have no need to go inside it. If I need anything, I send one of my staff.' He shrugged. 'You can check, if you like. You have my ID pass. See if you can run it through one of your software checks. You'll find it's never been used to gain access to the hangar.'

'But you know the sort of things that are in there?'

'I know some of the things,' said Gareth carefully.

'The Malichea Index?' asked Guy.

'I don't know,' replied Gareth.

'But it could be?' pressed Guy.

Gareth hesitated, then he admitted reluctantly, 'Yes, it could be.'

Guy smiled.

'That's good enough for me.' He turned to Patch and Midge and ordered, 'Untie the girl and take them all back down to the dungeons.'

As they untied Lauren, Guy told Jake warningly, 'I'm going to do some further checking on this Laker Heath place, Jake. If I think you're lying, or trying to set me up, you will all suffer more than you can ever imagine.'

After they had been pushed back into the cell, Jake gently removed the tape from Lauren's mouth and hugged her tightly.

'I really thought he was going to cut my fingers off,' she shuddered. 'I thought I was going to end up just like Jasper Brigstocke.'

'I wouldn't let that happen to you,' Jake reassured her.

'You wouldn't have had much choice,' said Lauren, still trembling. 'Not against that many. They're armed, remember.'

'What happened?' asked Dan.

Quickly, they told Dan what had taken place upstairs: the threats, and Jake's desperate attempt to put Guy off by suggesting The Index was hidden at Laker Heath.

'What made you mention Laker Heath?' asked Gareth, curious.

'It was a hunch,' said Jake. 'I'm so glad you backed me up.'

'I could tell you were up to something, but I couldn't work out what,' said Gareth. 'I guessed it was to play for time.'

'Right,' said Jake. 'I was thinking: if I can persuade Guy The Index is there, and I can get him away from here, hopefully going with me to Laker Heath, that might give you a chance to do something while we're gone. Overpower his crew when they come down. Get out of here.'

'That might be possible.' Gareth nodded. 'From what I can make out, Guy's the only one with a gun.'

'We saw Spider holding one when we saw them at de Courcey Hall,' pointed out Lauren.

'It could be the same gun,' said Jake thoughtfully. 'It was all part of a scam, anyway.'

'I'm pretty sure they've just got the one gun,' agreed Gareth. Then he added, 'You realise you won't be able to get into the hangar at Laker Heath, Jake. It needs Level Five security clearance at least, and there are lots of security precautions in place to stop unauthorised people getting access.'

'I know about fingerprint ID,' said Jake. 'But I don't need to get into the hangar. I don't even need to actually go to Laker Heath. All I want to do is get Guy away from here, and try and overpower him in some way, and then call up help. If you've been able to get out of here in the meantime, great. But, if not, I'll get reinforcements.' He looked at Gareth. 'Do you have a special number for me to call? And a code word?'

Gareth hesitated, and Jake could tell he was deliberating whether to reveal a top-secret code and contact.

'It's our only way out,' Jake urged him.

Gareth nodded. He gave Jake a three-digit number. Jake frowned.

'Is that all? Just three digits?'

'It's an emergency number,' said Gareth. 'Like 999. In an emergency, there's no time to start keying in a long sequence of numbers.'

'OK.' Jake nodded. 'At least it's easy to remember. And the code, to prove it's not a hoax when I call.'

'Pig seven,' said Gareth.

'Pig seven?' queried Jake.

'That's the current codeword. It's changed every month.'

'OK,' muttered Jake. He hugged Lauren tightly to him again as he said, 'Let's hope Guy takes the bait.'

It was another two hours before they heard footsteps on the stone steps, and Duke and Des appeared at the door of the cell. As before, Duke was carrying the machete, and he held it menacingly as Des unlocked the cell door.

'Guy wants you,' Des said to Jake. 'The rest of you, back away from the door.'

Lauren, Dan and Gareth moved to the back of the cell as Jake stepped forward, through the doorway. Des locked the door, then Jake followed Des up the steps. Duke followed behind, prodding Jake painfully with the point of the machete to remind him what would happen if he tried any tricks.

Guy was sitting at a laptop. Gadge, Midge and Patch stood behind him, looking over his shoulder, studying the screen.

Spider was sprawled across two chairs, his eyes closed, as if he was grabbing a nap.

'I've done some checking on this Laker Heath place you mentioned, Jake,' Guy said, gesturing at the laptop. 'The internet gossip, conspiracy websites, that sort of thing. I've also put in a few calls to some old school chums I haven't seen in years who seem to back up what you'd said about weird stuff being kept at this place. They also mentioned this aircraft hangar at the base as the place where things like that are kept.'

'Just like I said,' said Jake, feeling the relief creep in.

That feeling vanished with Guy's next words.

'The problem, these old school chums tell me, is that security is very tight there. You can get into the base with Level Three security clearance, but to get into the hangar needs clearance at a much higher level. According to a pal of mine, that needs Level Five. Do you have your work ID card on you, Jake?'

Jake hesitated, wondering whether to deny it, but what was the point? They'd just take his wallet off him and find it inside.

'Yes,' he said. He took his ID card out of his wallet and handed it to Guy. Guy studied it. The photo of Jake on the front. The black magnetic strip on the back. The number 3 in silver lettering next to Jake's photo.

'Security Level Three,' he said. 'So, you can get into the base, but you can't get into the hangar.'

'No,' said Jake.

'Which is a pity,' said Guy. 'Because there's only one way to find out if your theory is correct, Jake, and that's for you and me to go to this place and check.'

Then he smiled, and from his pocket he took another ID card, virtually identical to Jake's, except it had the number 5 in the same silver lettering on it.

'Luckily for us, your friend Gareth Findlay-Weston was carrying his ID card on him when we picked him up. Look, Jake. Level Five. That means, with this card, I can get us into that hangar.' He held it out towards Jake, and Jake could see that the photo of Gareth had been replaced with one of Guy.

'Good, isn't it,' said Guy. 'It's wonderful what you can do these days with digital technology.' Then he sighed. 'However, this old pal of mine I spoke to told me there was an extra-tight piece of security about these ID passes, especially when getting into a high-level security area like this hangar at Laker Heath. Do you know what that is, Jake?'

Jake felt his throat go dry and felt a sick feeling in the pit of his stomach.

'Yes,' he said in a quiet voice that was almost a whisper.

'And what is that extra piece of security?' asked Guy, putting on a casual, relaxed air.

He knows, thought Jake. He's playing with me.

'I'll tell you, shall I, Jake,' said Guy. 'It's a finger-print. Index finger, right hand. So, you can see the problem, Jake,' said Guy. 'The photo may be of me, but it won't match with my fingerprint.'

'I'll go there,' said Jake desperately. He had to keep Guy on track with the idea that The Index was at Laker Heath and give them time to work out how to get away. 'I'll go in.'

'But you can't get into the hangar,' said Guy. 'Not with a Level Three security pass. And I don't really trust you to go there on your own, Jake. You might not come back. You might run to the police, and tell them where we are.' He shook his head. 'No no, Jake, we can't have that. You and I shall go to this place together and see if The Index is there. This Level Five card will get

191

me in, and once I'm in, I'll sneak you in with me. So all I need to make it work is an index finger.' He smiled. 'One that matches the fingerprint they'll have on file for your friend, Gareth Findlay-Weston.

'Now I could take him with me. But the problem is he looks a bit battered and his appearance might raise some awkward questions. So I think it's safer for us if he stays here.' He picked up the machete and gently swung it in his hand. Then he turned to Spider and Duke. 'Spider, will you and Duke go down and bring Mr Findlay-Weston up here. I think he's got something that I need.' And he grinned.

# Chapter 23

Jake was still feeling sick as he, Guy and Des stepped outside the castle into the fresh air. Gareth had been brought up from the dungeons and tied to the same heavy wooden chair where Lauren had sat. And then Duke had cut off Gareth's index finger with a savage blow from the machete. Jake could still hear Gareth's scream as the blade slicked through his finger and bit into the wood of the chair. They hadn't bothered to use tape over his mouth to silence Gareth, as they had with Lauren.

'Ice and a plastic bag, please, Midge,' Guy had said, picking up Gareth's finger from the floor.

As Midge brought a paper cup and a plastic bag to Guy, Guy had grinned at Jake and said, 'Isn't it wonderful that these fast-food drive-throughs always give you too much ice with your drink!'

Then Guy had scooped the ice from the cup into the plastic bag, dropped Gareth's finger into it, and put it in his pocket, while Gareth was untied and dragged out of the room and back down to the dungeons.

'I think we're ready to go now, Jake,' said Guy.

Guy took the pistol from his pocket and showed it to Jake.

'Just to remind you I've got this, Jake. Try anything and you're dead. Remember, now I've got Mr Findlay-Weston's finger and his ID card, I can still get into that hangar with or without you. At the moment I need you because you know what you're looking for. But, at a pinch, I can try this without you. Just remember that.'

He slid the gun back into his coat pocket.

'Des, you keep an eye on things here.'

Des looked concerned.

'Don't you want me to drive?' he asked. 'Say he tries anything?'

Guy smiled confidently.

'He won't,' he assured Des. 'Because we're going to have an arrangement.' He turned to Jake and said, 'Just in case you're thinking that while we're away from here, it's worth trying to overpower me, or crash the car or something, and then get away and warn the authorities, that's not a good idea. You see, I'm leaving Des with specific instructions.' He looked at his watch. 'It's three o'clock now. It'll take us about an hour to get to Laker Heath. Let's be generous, say an hour and a half. Then half an hour inside to find The Index.' He grinned cockily. 'Let's be generous again. Forty-five minutes.' He turned to Des. 'So, Des, if you don't get a call from me by a quarter past five, you kill Jake's girlfriend and the other two.' He turned back to Jake. 'How does that sound to you, Jake? Think we'll have The Index by quarter past five?'

Jake stared at Guy, shocked, his mind reeling. Yes, Guy was mad.

'We don't even know it's there!' he protested.

'It was your guess, Jake,' said Guy. 'That's what saved your girlfriend.' He gave Jake a questioning look. 'If you're having second thoughts, we could always go back inside and . . .'

At the thought of Lauren tied to the chair, and the sound of the machete crunching through Gareth's finger, Jake shook his head.

'No,' he said quickly, feeling sick. 'I'm sure it's there.'

'Good,' said Guy. 'Right, Des. Expect a phone call from me by quarter past five. If you don't get it, kill them. Right, Jake, let's go and get the car. You first.'

'Where is it?' asked Jake. 'I didn't see any cars when we came.'

'That's because you came in the back way,' said Guy. 'The front entrance is this way.' And he pointed towards where the overgrown pathway headed towards a gap in the trees. Then he stopped, and dropped his hand, a startled expression on his face. Jake looked at what had made him stop, and saw that the three Mexicans who'd grabbed him and Lauren had just walked through this same gap and were standing glaring grimly at Guy.

'Manolo!' exclaimed Guy. The startled surprise had gone and been replaced by a friendly, cheerful tone of welcome. Yes, thought Jake ruefully, Guy really can switch his charm on and off. 'You found me!' Then, curious, he asked, 'How?'

'That's not important,' growled Manolo. He reached into his pocket and pulled a knife from it, the same knife he'd threatened Jake and Lauren with.

'Well, I disagree, old friend,' said Guy. 'It's important to me.'

'You cheat us!' snarled Manolo. 'You promise us money, but then you sell us out.'

'I did nothing of the sort!' protested Guy.

'Then where is money you promise us?' demanded the angry Mexican.

'I've got it safe,' said Guy. 'It's in a bank.'

Manolo scowled again.

'Money in a bank no good to us,' he grunted, and his two companions nodded. 'You promise us cash.'

'And you shall have cash,' Guy assured them, his voice sincere and earnest.

'When?' demanded the Mexican harshly.

'I can let you have some right now,' said Guy. 'Let's call it a down payment.'

'Let's see this money!' demanded Manolo suspiciously.

Guy nodded, put his hand into his coat pocket, and pulled out the gun. Before the Mexicans could react or take a cover, he pressed the trigger and a stream of bullets poured out, with Guy spraying the gunfire back and forth, left and right. It was over in seconds. Jake stared in horror at the bodies of the three dead Mexicans sprawled on the ground.

Guy took a fresh clip of ammunition from his pocket and replaced the empty clip in the gun, then put the weapon back in his pocket. He turned to Jake with a broad smile on his face.

'See, Jake!' he said. 'What did I tell you! The Hechler and Koch MP5K! A fantastic piece of kit!'

The sound of gunfire had brought the others out of the ruins. They stared at the bodies of the dead Mexicans.

'Nosy people,' explained Guy airily. 'They could have got us into trouble. You'd better get rid of them while Jake and I are away. Bury them somewhere. Oh, and you'd better go and find their car. Take it and set fire to it, but do it somewhere away from here. We don't want any more people sniffing around.'

He gestured at Jake.

'Right, Jake. Let's you and I do what we have to.' He looked at his watch. 'We lost a bit of time with that interruption, Des, so let's say we'll make it half past five before I call you. OK?'

Des nodded. Guy hesitated, and then he walked back to Des and whispered something in his ear. Des nodded. Guy smiled. Then he rejoined Jake.

'OK, Jake. Let's you and I head for Laker Heath.'

# Chapter 24

They were in the SUV with the blacked-out windows, on their way to the base at Laker Heath. Jake was driving. Guy sat directly behind him, the gun on his lap. 'Just to remind you, Jake,' Guy had warned him. 'Try anything odd, pulling over, using the flashers to attract attention, crashing the car, anything, and I pull the trigger and you're dead.'

Now, as Jake drove, he heard a metallic sound from behind him.

'What's going on?' he demanded suspiciously. 'What are you doing?'

'My, you do have sharp ears,' murmured Guy. 'I'm fitting a suppressor to the barrel of the gun.'

'Why?' asked Jake.

'Why?' repeated Guy. 'Honestly, Jake, for someone who's supposed to be intelligent, you do ask the most stupid questions. We're going to be in a hangar on a top-secret base. It's possible that we may run into trouble, and I may have to use this. In which case, the noise of the gun going off would draw attention to us, which is not something I want.' His tone changed to chattiness as he added, 'Just to clarify, a suppressor — or silencer as most people call them — doesn't actually completely eliminate the sound of the gun going off. It just reduces it. Did you know there are five different categories of gun noise? Action, blast, sonic signature, impact and operation. The two loudest noises are muzzle blast and sonic signature, and that's what this little baby deals with.' Jake heard the note that was almost one of affection in Guy's voice.

As he drove, Jake's mind was rapidly wondering how he could get out of this, what he could do to overpower Guy, get hold of the gun, and use it to threaten Guy. Order him to make that call to Des and call him off, or Jake would kill him. But that would be difficult, if not impossible, to do while they were driving. Especially because he had to keep their speed up. He couldn't afford to slow down, not if they were going to get to Laker Heath in an hour.

'I do hope you're right about The Index being there,' murmured Guy. 'It would be a great pity to have to kill your girlfriend. She seems like a very nice person.'

'How do I know you won't kill her anyway?' asked Jake. 'And me. And Dan and Gareth.'

He was remembering the callously indifferent way that Guy had killed the Mexicans. Killing people was nothing to him.

'Jake, I'm disappointed in you,' said Guy. 'I like you, Jake. You've been enormously helpful to me. Without you, I wouldn't have got this far.'

'That still doesn't mean you won't kill me,' said Jake.

In the rear-view mirror, Jake saw Guy shake his head, and heard him give a sigh of disappointment.

'You've got me all wrong, Jake,' he said. 'I only kill people who get in my way, or interfere with my plans. You're helping me, Jake. I have no reason to kill you.'

You have every reason, thought Jake bitterly. For one thing, I'm a witness to you killing those three Mexicans, and chopping off Gareth's finger, and everything else that's been going on. But it would be foolish to say those thoughts out loud, he thought. Better to let Guy think that he believed that Guy was going to let them all go, even though it was obviously a lie. Maybe because Guy was insane, he really believed he meant something at the time he said it. That was why he was so persuasive and believable with his charm. Perhaps the best thing was to lull Guy into a sense of relaxation, of confidence; and then grab him when the opportunity arose, when he had become too relaxed. Get him to talk. Get him to boast. People like Guy love

201

talking about themselves and how clever they think they are.

'One thing I don't understand, Guy,' he said. 'Why all these games?'

'Games?'

'You know, pretending to be trapped. Needing to be rescued. Why that business at de Courcey Hall with Spider holding that gun on you?'

Guy laughed.

'Yes, I thought that was clever,' he said. 'Though I must admit you began to worry me, taking so long to get there. Do you know how long we had to hang around in that car park waiting for you to arrive? You were so slow, so stupid, Jake! I'd worked out that the books might be in the old library ages before you did.'

'But why do it?'

'Because I needed you to think I was the victim here. And I needed you to keep telling the police that, while at the same time I was telling them I was fine. It's called confusion, Jake. And it also meant the police were getting more and more irritated by you, and more and more suspicious of what your motives were. You were my scapegoat, Jake, right from the very beginning. Even before I shot Alex Munro. I assume your friend, Mr Findlay-Weston, told you that was me.'

'Yes,' said Jake. 'But I don't know why you did it?'

'Like I said, I needed a scapegoat, someone to take the heat off me, and you were perfect for it.

'When Alex Munro contacted me to ask about The Index, and about the Order of Malichea, he told me there were three people who knew more about it than even he did. You, your girlfriend, and Gareth Findlay-Weston of MI5, whose cover was as the Head of the Department of Science Press Department. I must admit I thought it was a bit strange him telling me all this, but I discovered that was his style: a pretend openness. Telling me the bits he thought might pull me in.

'Unfortunately, by doing that he was signing his own death warrant. Once I knew that, and that Munro didn't have the information, I decided to bring you into the game. But as Munro had already told me you were a wild card, you had to be handled with caution. So, I decided to put you in the frame for killing Munro. Along with me, of course. I thought that would make sure we met.'

'How were you able to shoot Munro?' asked Jake. 'He always had bodyguards with him.'

'I set up a situation where he'd make a good target,' said Guy. 'I'm a pretty good shot. I was brought up to shoot. I've been using a rifle since I was eight.' He grinned. 'Being able to handle a gun has got me out of trouble on more than one occasion. It was a diffi-cult shot. I guessed it had to be a head shot just in

case Munro was wearing body armour, or something.'
He chuckled. 'It was perfect. His head exploded like a
melon!'

'So that was you who sent me the text about meeting at Muswell Hill?'

'Of course.'

'How did you manage to get my name along with
yours into his schedule for the meeting at Crouch End?
I suppose you hacked into his diary?'

'No need,' said Guy. 'I told him I'd been in touch
with you, and you had agreed to come along. Much
simpler. He was very pleased.'

'What about the Mexicans?'

Guy grinned.

'Ah, the Mexicans!' He smiled nostalgically. 'Manolo,
Pedro and Almador. Wonderful chaps! It was them I was
working with when I landed in jail in Mexico.' He chuckled. 'Well, when I say "working with", what I really
mean is, I was ripping them off. Unfortunately for me,
they found out about it, so when they discovered I was
going to be released, they pointed out to me that I
owed them.' He shrugged ruefully. 'And they didn't
mean just the money I'd planned to take off them.
They meant my life.' He gave a shrug. 'Injured macho
pride. Revenge. Whatever you like to call it, it meant
the same thing. They wanted the money I'd promised
them, and then they were going to kill me.'

He let out an unhappy sigh and fell silent.

'So?' prompted Jake quickly, desperate to keep him talking.

'So, when they realised that I was involved in something back in England that could mean big bucks, mucho dollars, they insisted they come along too. They saw me as an investment. Of course, I was happy to go along with that until we got back here.' He chuckled. 'Believe me, Jake, if I hadn't gone along with it, I wouldn't have got out of Mexico alive.'

'And, once you were in England, you double-crossed them.'

'They were going to kill me, Jake!'

'And what about Pierce Randall?'

'Ah, yes. Pierce Randall!' And Jake could hear the smile in Guy's voice. 'The most powerful firm of lawyers in the world! People who think they have absolute power are always the easiest to fool.'

'How did you do it? Manage to convince the police you were with Pierce Randall, while you weren't?'

'But I was working with them, Jake!' said Guy, his voice full of fake protest. Then he chuckled. 'At least, they thought I was. Remember, I was bailed into their custody, but that didn't mean I had to stay with them. And, because Pierce Randall were keen to keep me happy, because they wanted me to find The Index for them, they let me do my own thing as far as where I stayed while I was out on bail.' He laughed again. 'All right, I wasn't exactly *honest* with them about where I was, or what I was up to, but these are lawyers. And with very dubious morals, as I'm sure you know. So you could say I played them at their own game.'

'How?' asked Jake.

Guy gave a pretend weary sigh.

'If we had time I'd tell you every little bit of how I played everyone off against one another,' he said smugly.

'We've got time,' said Jake.

'True, but I don't feel like it,' said Guy. 'And you would surely feel very embarrassed about how I'd made a fool of you. Like that message on your window when you and your girlfriend got back to your flat.'

'That was you?'

'Midge. Very good with locks.'

'So you'd set all this up long before we met at that police cell?'

'Of course,' said Guy. 'Almost from the first time I heard from poor Alex Munro.'

'Was it you and your crew who killed Jasper Brigstocke?' asked Jake. 'You tortured him and killed him.'

'I didn't kill him,' protested Guy. 'I wanted to keep him alive so he could give me the answer I wanted.'

'Like, who he'd sold the books to?'

'Exactly. But he kept insisting he didn't even have them.'

'So who did kill him?'

'No one. His heart gave out.'

'And you cutting his fingers off and torturing him had nothing to do with that?'

'It was a chance I took,' said Guy. 'The prize is worth it.'

'The Index.'

'Exactly,' said Guy. 'What was it you said when we were in that police cell? It's worth billions.' He smiled. 'Don't you just love that word: *billions*! Oh, I do hope it's there at Laker Heath, Jake. For *all* our sakes.'

# Chapter 25

It was 16:45 when they reached the gates of Laker Heath base. Just forty-five minutes before Des kills Lauren and the others, thought Jake, a sick feeling going from deep in the pit of his stomach right up to his throat.

'Not bad,' said Guy. 'Though I thought you'd have made it here a bit quicker, in view of the clock ticking on your girlfriend's life.'

Laker Heath was the same as Jake remembered it from when he'd come here on a training course. The base was spread over a huge area, like a military camp. And, as with many military camps, it was protected by a high wire fence, topped with razor wire.

There was one main gate in, and as Jake headed for it, he hoped the security was still the same as it had been the last time he was here. Then all it had needed was a check of the ID card. The tighter security, requiring the additional fingerprint ID, was only a requirement for anyone intending to access the large hangar-like building at the other side of the base.

Jake pulled the SUV to a halt by the yellow metal barrier across the main entrance and wound down his window. Behind him, Guy did the same. There were two soldiers inside the security cabin, one at the window, one inside. Jake took out his ID card and held it out to the soldier in the cabin.

Please don't let them ask for fingerprint ID, he prayed silently. He was sure Guy would find a way to fool them, using Gareth's finger, but he didn't want there to be a chance for things to go wrong even before they'd got into the base. One step at a time, he told himself, trying to keep calm. First, get through this gate. Then, get past security into the hangar. Then . . . play it by ear. If there's no sign of The Index, over-power Guy, take his gun off him, and force him to make that phone call.

The soldier took Jake's ID card, compared the photo on it with Jake himself, then handed the card back to him. The soldier did the same with the ID card that Guy handed to him. A button was pressed inside the security cabin, and the barrier rose up.

Jake drove the SUV through the main gate, and towards where he knew the hangar to be.

'So far so good,' murmured Guy behind him.

Jake continued along the main road through the base, passing single-storey buildings, all identified with letters: AA, AB, AC . . . CD, CE, CF . . .

'You've been here before,' commented Guy.

'A long time ago,' said Jake. 'And only on the outer part of the base.'

'But you know where this hangar is?'

'Yes,' said Jake. He gestured ahead. 'In fact, you can see it, past the next load of buildings.'

'Ah yes,' said Guy.

The hangar was huge. It towered above the rest of the base like a pyramid rising from the sands of ancient Egypt.

'Where's the security around it?' asked Guy, and Jake could hear the impatience in his voice.

'We're about to get to it,' said Jake.

He took a left, then a right, and they saw in front of them the double-wire fence topped with razor wire protecting the hangar. There was a security checkpoint at a gate in the fence, leading into the inner security area, and the hangar. This security checkpoint was more fortified than the cabin at the main gate into the base. Instead of a metal barrier, there were two large and very heavy metal gates. Razor wire not only topped the fence and the gates, but was woven in between the wires of the fence. Concrete blocks had been placed in a zigzag pattern at strategic points leading up to the checkpoint so that the gate couldn't be rammed. As well as the soldiers they could see on duty inside the checkpoint cabin, two heavily armed soldiers stood on either side of the gate.

'Pull over,' snapped Guy.

Jake pulled the car to a halt.

'What now?' he asked.

'Swing back and pull up in a sheltered area near one of the buildings,' ordered Guy. 'Out of sight of that checkpoint.'

Jake turned the SUV and drove back, heading towards the main gate.

'There, on the left,' said Guy.

There was a car park on the left, behind one of the low buildings. Jake turned the SUV into it.

'OK,' mused Guy thoughtfully. 'If they use the finger-print ID check at that gate, this could be a problem. I should be able to get through there with Level Five clearance, but you definitely won't.'

'So I'll drop you off and wait for you here,' said Jake.

Guy scowled.

'If you test my patience with that kind of asinine crack again, Jake, I'll shoot you without further thought. You are not leaving my sight until all this is over.'

'So what do we do?'

'We get out of the car and you get in the boot. There's a nice little space there under the carpet. I'll drive us

211

through using your friend's Level Five pass. Once we're in, you can get out from the boot. And don't try shouting out any warnings. Remember, if I don't make that call, your girlfriend dies.'

'I remember,' grunted Jake.

Jake and Guy got out. Jake went to the boot, opened it, and lifted up the carpet. As Guy had said, there was a perfect empty space beneath it. Jake guessed that it had been used before for smuggling things in and out of places: people, contraband.

Jake climbed in and curled himself up into the hole, and Guy pulled the carpet over him, covering him.

'Remember,' warned Guy, his voice now muffled by the carpet, 'no tricks.'

Jake felt the car shudder as the boot slammed shut, then he heard Guy clamber into the driving seat. The car started up, and moved off.

The space was small and cramped. Jake was already feeling pain in his back from where he was bent double to fit into it, but he knew he daren't make any noises or movements to try and stretch and ease his discomfort.

Would they get through? Would the soldiers on duty believe Guy? Would Guy be able to use Gareth's finger on the fingerprint ID without his sleight of hand being spotted? How? What if the soldiers on duty got suspicious and made Guy open the boot, and they peeled back the carpet and found Jake?

The thought of all the things that could go wrong made Jake feel sick.

The car stopped and Jake heard one of the soldiers say, 'We saw you pull up before. What happened to you?'

Jake heard Guy's voice, cheerful and chatty, friendly as ever, as he said, 'I had to drop my pal off.'

'OK,' grunted the soldier. 'ID?'

'Here,' said Guy.

Jake could imagine him handing over Gareth's ID card, and the soldier studying it.

'OK,' said the soldier. 'Fingerprint on the glass screen.'

There was silence, and Jake's heart was in his mouth as he imagined the scene outside the car, as the soldier held out the ID machine to Guy. Guy surely couldn't produce the remains of a bloody finger and press it against an ID screen in front of the soldier!

There was a heart-stopping pause that seemed to go on for ages. Then Jake heard the sound of machinery activating as the gates opened, and the soldier said, 'OK. Go through.'

Jake felt the SUV move forward. He heard the gates shut heavily behind them. They travelled for a few moments, and then the car stopped. Jake heard the driver's door open and close, and then the sound of the boot being opened. The carpet was peeled back, and Jake looked up into Guy's face.

'Easier than I thought,' said Guy, smirking. 'Your friend's finger worked a treat.'

As Jake got out of the back of the car, he saw that Guy had parked next to a high-sided van, which kept them out of sight from the security checkpoint gate. They were right beside a door set into the wall of the hangar. Next to the door was an ID scanner, with a slot for the ID card, and another screen for the fingerprint check.

'How did you do it?' asked Jake, stunned. 'You can't have just pulled a bloody finger out of your pocket!'

'Credit me with some intelligence!' snapped Guy irritably. 'They had one of these mirror pads, like a mobile phone screen. He handed it to me through the car window. I dropped it, accidentally on purpose, into the footwell of the car, and while I was picking it up off the floor, I pressed Mr Findlay-Weston's finger against the screen. Hey presto! Open sesame!' He looked up at the massive shape of the hangar and muttered, 'So far so good, Jake. Right, this is the last stage. Let's hope our luck continues, because if The Index *isn't* in here, things are going to go very bad.'

# Chapter 26

As they walked towards the door, Guy ordered, 'Stay close to me, Jake, so that when the door opens we both get through. It might be on a timer that shuts as soon as one person walks through it.'

Jake shot a look at his watch. 17:00 hours. They had less than thirty minutes to find The Index so that Guy could make the call. Once again, Jake did his best to try and keep himself calm. Inside, he knew this was a dead end, despite the confidence with which he'd told Guy that The Index would be here. It was now just a matter of waiting for the right moment to grab Guy and take his gun off him. Maybe he should have raised the alarm at the checkpoint? The soldiers would have overpowered Guy. But his fear was that Guy would have pulled out his own gun, a fire-fight would have taken place, and Guy would have been shot dead. Jake needed him alive.

And even if the soldiers had been able to take Guy alive, wounded or otherwise, there was no guarantee that Guy would make that phone call to save Lauren and the others. The soldiers wouldn't necessarily believe Jake's story either. And, even if they did, they'd hardly be likely to threaten to kill Guy unless he made the phone call. No, only Jake would be able to do that, which meant Jake was on his own. He had to overpower Guy. Maybe when they were going through this door together?

Jake stopped by the door with Guy close behind him. With one hand in his jacket pocket, holding the gun on Jake, Guy used his free hand to push Gareth's ID card through the scanner. Then he took Gareth's finger from his pocket and pressed the tip against the glass screen.

There was a click and the door opened.

Guy pushed Jake and the two of them slipped through the doorway like one person, then the door shut, and they were inside the hangar. Jake was scanning the warehouse for a weapon but all he could see were rows and rows of shelves in aisles, reaching up to the curved ceiling. Above each aisle was a letter, all neatly alphabetised: A, B, C . . . And every shelf in every row looked to be packed with items, boxed or wrapped up.

'We're in!' murmured Guy. 'Right, Jake, what next?'

A noise made them turn round. An armed soldier was approaching them, his gun pointing towards them. Jake had blown his moment.

'Let's see your ID cards,' snapped the soldier.

'But we've just used them to get in!' protested Guy.

'You know the rules,' said the soldier. 'Triple protection. Gate security, door security, and the final face-to-face check.' He frowned suspiciously. 'But the fact you don't know . . .'

'Yes, all right,' grumbled Guy. 'They told us back at the office. But this is our first time, and I'd forgotten.'

The soldier still regarded them warily.

'Where is your office?'

Guy shot a look at Jake, who said, 'The Department of Science press office in Marsham Street.'

The soldier didn't look convinced. He held out his hand.

'Let's see your ID cards,' he said.

Guy held out Gareth's ID card.

The soldier studied it, comparing the photo with Guy. Then he ran it through a decoding machine on the wall beside the door. The machine beeped.

'OK.' The soldier nodded. He held out a small machine, similar to a mobile phone. 'Right index finger on the screen.'

Guy reached out to take it, and as he did he suddenly produced a knife from behind his back with his other hand and thrust it upwards hard beneath the soldier's chin. The blade hit the soft flesh and sank in deep, upwards. The soldier's eyes opened wide in shock, his mouth dropped open and blood gushed out. Then he crumpled against Guy.

Guy pushed the dead soldier away, pulling his long-bladed knife out from beneath the soldier's chin. Guy wiped the blade, closed it, and reached round the back of his jacket, slipping the knife into a hidden pocket.

'Always keep a knife behind your back where you can get hold of it quickly in an emergency, Jake,' he said almost casually. 'A gun's very effective, but the last thing we want is a gun going off, even with a suppressor fitted, that might bring people running.'

Jake stared at the dead soldier.

'Come on,' said Guy. 'Get him out of sight, in case anyone else turns up.'

Jake looked at Guy. He was still in a state of shock.

'Come on!' snapped Guy urgently. 'I don't need to tell you the clock is ticking, if you want to save your girlfriend!'

This could be my chance, thought Jake. He gestured at the dead body of the soldier.

'I can't move him on my own,' he said.

Guy shook his head.

'Do it!' he snapped. 'Or else I might think you're trying to distract me.'

Jake hesitated, then grabbed the dead body of the soldier by the ankles and dragged it over to a small table near the door.

'Put his gun with him,' ordered Guy. He pointed to a roll of tarpaulin. 'Then cover him with that tarp.'

Jake did as he was ordered, snatching a glance at his watch. 17:05. Twenty-five minutes to go.

Guy saw him look at his watch and chuckled.

'Yes, indeed, Jake. Time is passing. So, let's find this book. Where do we start?'

'I don't know,' admitted Jake helplessly. 'I've never been in here before.'

'Then *think*, Jake. It's worked for you so far. That's what's got us here.'

'Well, the boxes seem to be in alphabetical order,' said Jake.

'Good.' Guy nodded. 'So, we're looking for The Index. Under I, do you reckon?'

'No,' said Jake, shaking his head. 'M for Malichea. If it's here, that's where it'll be.'

'It had better be here,' said Guy menacingly. 'You know what's at risk if it isn't.'

'It'll be here,' Jake reassured him desperately.

Jake hurried to the aisle of shelves with a big 'M' above it, and began to work his way along the row, scanning, looking particularly for anything with the familiar black leather covering with the letter 'M' and the symbol of the Order embossed on it. There were plenty of labels beginning with 'Ma . . .', but nothing that looked like anything Jake could connect with the Order of Malichea.

There *has* to be something here, he thought. There should be at least *one* of the books, and more! But there was nothing. The files labelled 'Ma . . .' became files and packets marked 'Mb . . .'.

Jake turned on Guy, who glared at him grimly.

'Well?' demanded Guy, his voice like ice.

'I don't know!' said Jake helplessly. 'There should be *something* here! I know for sure that Gareth and his people have found some of the hidden books, so they should be here!'

'But they're not,' snapped Guy. He pulled the gun from his pocket. 'It looks like you tried to con me, Jake. I warned you what would happen if you did that . . .'

'No!' burst out Jake, as a sudden realisation hit him. 'Sigma!'

'What?' queried Guy, puzzled.

'I've just remembered, that's one of the code words they used for stuff like the hidden books. We're in the wrong place! We should be where the S files are!'

Guy scowled.

'I get the definite feeling you're just playing for time,' he grated. 'Well, your time has run out!'

And he levelled the gun at Jake.

'Wait!' appealed Jake. 'Follow me!'

And he hurried off towards the aisle with a big 'S' above it, all the time expecting to get a bullet in the back. Instead, he heard Guy's footsteps hurry after him. As Jake ran, he looked again at his watch. Ten past. Twenty minutes.

Jake reached the aisle marked 'S' and rushed down it, scanning the shelves hurriedly, aware that if there was nothing here he had no choice but to try and throw himself at Guy and attempt to wrestle the gun off him.

He ran down the aisle, his eye running over the labels as he did, and suddenly he saw them. The familiar leather-wrapped objects, with the Malichea symbol. There were about twenty of them, all different sizes.

'There!' he said triumphantly.

Guy joined him.

'Which one is The Index?' he asked.

'I don't know,' admitted Jake. 'My guess is it would look like the *Journal*, that sort of size.'

'So what are these?' demanded Guy.

'Some of them will be the books that have been found and brought here,' said Jake.

'OK, start opening them,' said Guy.

Jake shook his head.

'That's too dangerous. Some of the books contain traps to protect the information that's in them. The

221

only answer is to take all of them with us and find out which one is The Index later.'

Guy looked at the packets suspiciously.

'Say none of them are The Index?' he queried. 'Say these are just books with weird sciences in them?'

'They'll still be worth a fortune,' urged Jake. 'Each book will contain secrets that could be patented.'

'I don't want just a few of the books!' growled Guy. 'I want The Index. I want to know where *all* of them are! You promised me The Index, Jake!' He shook his head. 'I'll take these, but that wasn't our bargain!'

Once again he levelled the gun at Jake, and all Jake could think of was that it had all been in vain. He was going to die. Lauren was going to die.

'No!' he begged, and he half turned, flinching away from the bullet he knew would be coming, and as he did so he saw the brown paper package with 'Malichea — The Index' written on it in faded letters.

# Chapter 27

'It's here!' he breathed.

'What?' queried Guy, suspicion still in his voice.

'The Index!' exclaimed Jake. He pointed a trembling finger at the package. 'Look! There! They've even labelled it!' He took the package off the shelf and held it out towards Guy, so he could see the lettering on it.

Guy snatched the package from Jake, his eyes lighting up with greed.

'This is it!' he said, awed. 'The Index!'

'Make the phone call!' begged Jake. 'You promised!'

The thought of the phone call jerked Guy back into the present.

'Once we're back outside,' he snapped.

'That wasn't part of the deal!' protested Jake desperately.

'I'm the one with the gun, Jake,' said Guy menacingly. 'I say the terms of the deal.' He gestured at the leather-bound Malichea books on the shelf. 'Grab those and bring them with us.'

Jake scooped the Malichea books up in his arms.

'OK,' said Guy. 'Let's go.'

They ran back to the side door through which they'd come in. All the time, Jake was expecting someone to appear and gun them down, but it seemed there was only the one soldier on duty at a time actually inside the hangar. It made sense; with the high levels of security checking people coming in, it was highly unlikely the wrong people would be able to make it inside. Except today. Today, he and Guy had got in, and they had The Index. Now all they had to do was get out, and Lauren would be saved.

There were no security checks needed to get back out into the open, no ID scanners, no fingerprint checks.

'OK,' said Guy once they were outside. 'Get back into the boot. The guards only saw one of us drive in, we don't want to raise suspicion by them seeing two of us going out.'

Jake threw the Malichea books on the back seat, then opened the boot, peeled back the carpet, and climbed into the small space. Guy pulled the carpet over him.

Jake heard Guy getting into the car and the engine starting up. Then it began to move forward, stopping shortly afterwards. Jake heard the exchange between the soldiers on duty and Guy, with Guy sounding as relaxed as ever. Again, there were no fingerprint checks needed to get out, just a quick flash of the ID card Guy was carrying; and then there was the sound of mechanics as the gate swung open, and the car drove through.

The car drove for a short way, and pulled up.

Maybe he's making that phone call? thought Jake desperately. But instead he heard the boot open and the carpet was peeled back. Guy stood there, holding the gun. They were in the same car park where they'd parked before.

'Right, Jake. Get back in the driving seat. The guards saw you driving me in the main gate, so we'll let them see the same thing going out. You at the wheel. Me in the back. Again, there's no sense in having them asking awkward questions about what happened to you, and where you were dropped off.'

'The phone call to Des,' said Jake urgently. He showed Guy his watch. 'It's twenty-three minutes past. Seven minutes.'

'It'll be fine,' Guy told him reassuringly. 'In two minutes we'll be out through the main gate. I saw a lay-by about a hundred metres away from the main gate as we drove in. It's sheltered by trees. Pull up there. I'll make the call from there.'

Jake jumped behind the steering wheel of the SUV. Seven minutes! He prayed they wouldn't be held up going through the main gate.

Guy got into the back, the gun cradled in his hand. Jake guessed The Index was next to him on the seat.

'Just remember, I've got the gun trained on you, just like before,' Guy reminded him. 'And you need me to make that call.'

'No tricks,' Jake assured him.

Jake drove back along the main route of the base, fighting the urge to go at speed, but desperate not to be stopped for breaking the 10 mph speed limit. They reached the main gate, and the barrier.

Once again, Jake and Guy showed their ID cards to the soldier on duty in the cabin. Jake shot a glance at the clock in the dashboard. 17:26. Four minutes to go.

Raise the barrier! he begged silently. Instead, the soldier inside the cabin turned and began to talk to his companion.

No! thought Jake. Stop talking! Raise the barrier!

The clock moved to 17:27. Three minutes to go!

Jake was about to lower his window and shout at the soldier, but before he could, the soldier pressed a button, and the barrier rose. Jake drove the SUV through.

A lay-by, Guy had said. A hundred metres from the main gate. Shielded by trees. Where was it?

Then he saw it.

He pulled the car into the lay-by and turned urgently to Guy.

'The phone call!'

'Of course.' Guy nodded. 'OK. Get out of the car.'

'Why?' demanded Jake.

'Because I need you at a safe distance from me while I make the call,' said Guy. 'And even with a gun in my hand pointed at you, I don't trust you, Jake. I think once I've made the call, you'll try and jump me.'

'Make the call!' begged Jake.

'Out of the car!' repeated Guy.

Jake pushed open the door and stumbled out. Guy stepped out of the rear of the car, moving back from Jake, keeping a safe distance between them. He had his gun in his hand, but no phone.

'Your phone!' urged Jake. 'You've got The Index! Make the call!'

Guy sighed and shook his head. 'It'll be a waste of time, Jake. They're dead already.'

'No!' shouted Jake. He held his watch out towards Guy. 'There's still one minute!'

Guy shook his head again.

'You really are so gullible, Jake,' he said sadly. 'That business of my crew at the castle waiting for a phone call from me not to kill them. Why would I be stupid enough to let them go free? They can tell everyone about me, and about what happened.' He shook his head. 'Sorry, Jake. She's dead. That's what I whispered to Des, just before we left. I told my people to kill her after we'd gone, along with your boss, Gareth Findlay-Weston, and poor old Dan, and then clear out.'

Jake felt himself tremble, and he battled to stop himself shaking.

'You're lying!' he snapped.

'Why would I lie about that?' Guy shrugged. 'All I was ever after was The Index. Now I've got it, thanks to you. As long as you and your girlfriend, and Findlay-Weston, and even Dan, are all alive, you're a danger to me. In the old clichéd phrase, you know too much. You were always going to die.'

'No!' roared Jake, filled with more pain and anger than he'd ever known in his whole life. He threw himself forward at Guy, just as Guy fired. Jake felt the bullet pluck at his clothes and then felt a searing pain in his shoulder, but by then he was on Guy, grabbing for his gun-hand. The force of his rush brought both of them crashing down as Guy fired again, the bullet this time going harmlessly up into the late-afternoon sky.

Desperately, Jake held on to the wrist of Guy's gun-hand with one hand, forcing the barrel of the gun away from him, while with his other hand he grabbed Guy around the throat, trying to choke him. Guy brought up his knee sharply into Jake's groin, and the sudden pain made him release his hold on Guy's throat.

Guy smashed his head forward, butting Jake full in the face, and Jake felt blood pour from his nose.

Guy tried head-butting Jake again, but this time Jake jerked his head to one side, and Guy's head thudded into Jake's shoulder.

Jake turned his head, seizing Guy's ear between his teeth, and bit hard, while at the same time scrabbling with his free hand for the gun, desperate to wrench it out of Guy's hand. Guy howled with pain, and then kneed Jake in the groin again. A sick feeling surged through Jake, and for a second he lost his grip on Guy's gun-hand. Frantically, Jake grabbed for the pistol again, but Guy was too fast, and he used the gun as a club, smashing it into Jake's face. Another strike from the gun, this one to the side of Jake's neck, made him reel. He was aware of Guy struggling to his feet, and then standing, pointing the gun down at him. Jake tried to struggle to his feet, but a kick from Guy struck him hard on the side of the head, and he went down again. He tried to claw his way up, tried to leap at Guy, but Guy had moved back out of range, and now the gun was trained firmly on Jake.

Guy grinned vindictively.

'Goodbye, Jake,' he purred. 'It was interesting knowing you.'

A shot rang out and instinctively Jake closed his eyes . . .

Nothing happened. There was no tearing pain, no shattering thud as a bullet tore into him. Instead, Jake heard a crashing sound. He opened his eyes and saw Guy on his knees, his mouth and eyes wide open in shock. There was the sound of another shot, and then Guy fell face forward on to the ground.

# Chapter 28

Everything happened fast in the next few moments: a man completely covered from head to foot in black, and holding an automatic rifle, appeared, pointing the rifle at Jake. Jake felt his arms being grabbed and himself being lifted up off the ground, and then he was being hurried towards a large van. He was aware of another man, also dressed in black, standing nearby, his automatic rifle trained on him.

Special forces, realised Jake.

As Jake and the special forces soldier neared the van, the rear doors swung open, and Jake found himself being bundled into the back. He was shoved towards a wooden bench and pushed down on to it. Then three black-clad soldiers clambered in and sat down, one opposite and two sitting one on either side of him.

The last thing he saw was a black-clad soldier stand-ing over Guy's still body, then the rear doors slammed shut, and the van moved off.

'What's happening?' asked Jake. 'Where are we going?'

'Shut up,' grunted one of the soldiers tersely.

'Do you know Lauren? Is she all right?'

The soldier opposite him shook his head.

'Don't know who you're talking about,' he said.

'But . . .' appealed Jake.

'No questions,' snapped one of the soldiers beside him.

Jake shut up.

They rescued me, so they must be all right, he told himself.

But where was Lauren? Was she safe?

The journey took over an hour, the van shaking the whole while as it raced along. During that time the soldiers didn't exchange a word with Jake, or with one another.

Finally, the van pulled up. The rear doors opened and a tall man in a dark suit looked in.

'Welcome, Mr Wells,' he said in friendly tones. 'You can get out now.'

Bewildered, Jake stumbled out of the van. He looked around and saw he was in an underground car park.

The man shut the rear door, and the van raced off, heading for the exit.

'Who are you?' asked Jake.

'You may call me Gerald. Think of me as a friend,' said the man.

'Where's Lauren?' demanded Jake desperately.

Gerald nodded. 'She's fine. You'll see her in a moment. Please follow me.'

Jake followed Gerald to a lift, the door of which was already open. Jake hesitated.

'You're quite safe,' the man reassured him.

Gerald stepped into the lift, and Jake followed.

'Second floor,' said Gerald, and a mechanised electronic voice repeated: 'Second floor.'

Then the door closed and the lift rose.

Jake stepped out of the lift, and found himself face to face with a uniformed police officer, holding an automatic rifle.

'Pig seven,' said Gerald calmly, and the police officer stepped to one side and took up a position beside the lift.

Jake followed his escort along a corridor lined with numbered doors. I'm in an apartment block, he realised.

Gerald stopped by a door and rang the bell. The door opened, and Lauren looked out, apprehensive and nervous, until she saw Jake, and then her face broke into a huge smile of relief.

'Jake!' she burst out.

'I'll leave you two,' said the man who called himself Gerald. 'I'm sure you've got some catching up to do. If you need anything, just use the phone.'

With that, he turned and headed back along the corridor towards the lift. Jake stepped into the flat, and into Lauren's arms, and they hugged as if their lives had unexpectedly come back to them.

'So, what is this place?' asked Jake.

'It's an MI5 safe house,' said Lauren.

Lauren had patched up Jake's cuts and bruises, and now they were sitting in the very comfortable living room, drinking coffee.

'How did you get here?' asked Jake. 'How did you and Gareth and Dan get out of there?'

'Special forces,' said Lauren. She shook her head. 'I still don't know how they found us, and I don't think Gareth does, either. Although I didn't see much of him afterwards. They took him off to hospital.'

'But how did they know where to find you?' persisted Jake. 'They'd smashed our mobile phones. No one knew where Gareth was, or you, or me.'

'I don't know,' Lauren admitted. 'All I do know is that we were in that dungeon, and I was thinking of you at Laker Heath, and terrified about what was going to happen to you, and then suddenly we heard an explosion and gunfire from upstairs, and then these special forces types came down into the dungeon and released us.'

'The kids?'

'Locked up. But not before the explosion we heard freaked them all out. It was some kind of stun grenade going off.'

'And then?'

'And then I was brought here. I asked everyone what had happened to you, but no one would tell me.'

'Oh, I was OK,' said Jake.

'No you weren't!' burst out Lauren angrily. 'You went off with Guy to a place where you knew they didn't have The Index. You nearly got killed!'

'The Index was there,' said Jake.

Lauren stared at him.

'What?' she said, surprised.

'It's true,' said Jake. 'I held it in my hand.'

Lauren continued to stare, awed.

'The Index?' she stressed. 'The actual book itself?'

'Yes.'

Lauren grabbed him tightly to her.

'I was sure you were dead!' she said. 'I was certain he'd kill you when he found out you were just guessing, and there was no Index!'

'Well, I'm here!' Jake reminded her.

'Yes, but . . .' Lauren shook her head. 'I still don't understand how that happened.'

'Nor do I,' said Jake. 'But hopefully someone will tell us.'

# Chapter 29

The flat was well stocked, and the next morning they were able to prepare breakfast for themselves. No sooner had they finished than there was a ring at the door. Jake opened it. His escort from the previous night, Gerald, was standing there.

'I hope you had a good night's rest,' he said. 'Mr Findlay-Weston would like to see you. When you're ready, I'll take you to him.'

'We're ready now,' said Jake. The sooner we get to the bottom of this, the better, he thought.

Jake and Lauren followed Gerald back down to the underground car park, passing the armed police officer on duty at the lift. A car was waiting for them, a Merc.

'A bit more luxurious than the last vehicle I was here in,' observed Jake.

They drove through parts of London Jake didn't recognise, until they neared an area he did.

'We're in Greenwich,' he said. He pointed out through the window. 'There's the Royal Observatory. And the park.'

The car zigzagged through some quiet side streets, until it pulled into the car park outside a small building, with a sign that read: 'Lansdowne Medical Centre'.

'Gareth?' asked Jake.

'He's been undergoing some treatment,' said Gerald.

'Is he all right?' asked Lauren.

'I'll let Mr Findlay-Weston tell you that himself,' he replied.

He opened the doors for them, then headed towards the main entrance. As they followed him, Jake noticed that, as at the safe house, there was an armed police officer on duty.

Gerald flashed an ID card at the officer, who stepped aside and let them enter.

Inside, the building was like a small cottage hospital, but very high-tech. Lots of medical apparatus and staff, but no sign of the usual waiting areas.

It's a hospital for top-level security cases, realised Jake. People like Gareth.

They walked along a narrow corridor until they came to a door marked '5'. Gerald tapped at the door, and then opened it.

Jake and Lauren saw Gareth lying in a hospital bed,

attached to a monitor. The big surprise was seeing Sue Clark sitting on a chair beside Gareth's bed. She got up as she saw them, and headed for the door.

'Hi,' said Jake.

Clark nodded briefly in greeting, unsmiling, then brushed past them and walked away, towards the exit.

'I'll leave you together,' said Gerald, pushing the door shut.

'How are you?' asked Jake.

Gareth gave a smile.

'Take no notice of all this paraphernalia,' he said, gesturing at the medical equipment. 'I'm perfectly fine, but the powers-that-be won't believe me until the medics tell them I am. Please, sit down.'

'We haven't bought any grapes or anything,' said Jake. 'We didn't know where we were going.' Then, anxiously, he asked, 'Are you going to be all right?'

'According to the doctors, a few days' rest and I'll be fine.' He looked at his bandaged hand and sighed. 'Of course, I shall always be missing a finger, but that's a small price to pay for being alive.'

'What was Sue Clark doing here?' asked Lauren.

'I asked her to come and see me,' said Gareth.

'She didn't seem very friendly today,' observed Lauren.

'Don't be too condemning of her,' said Gareth. 'She saved your lives. And mine.'

Jake and Lauren looked at Gareth, puzzled.

'How?' asked Jake. 'Guy smashed our phones. There was no way to trace us.'

'Dan's sister, Gemma,' said Gareth.

Suddenly Jake realised. 'Gemma went to see Sue Clark!'

'And Sue Clark offered her money if she would keep an eye on you and report back to her what was going on.'

'Gemma would be good at that,' said Lauren. 'Dan told us she is always eavesdropping.' She smiled. 'I think she'd make a good spy.'

Gareth didn't smile at the suggestion.

'It seems that Gemma stayed in a Pierce Randall flat in London overnight, and then returned to Sevenoaks. She got Dan's message telling her you were all going to Platt Castle, so she went along in the hope of seeing what you were up to. She arrived in time to find Guy's crew burying three bodies.

'Then she phoned Sue Clark to tell her what was happening, and where. She told Ms Clark there was no sign of any of you at the place, but she'd found Dan's motorbike.'

'She thought the bodies were us!' exclaimed Lauren.

'At first.' Gareth nodded. 'But, after the kids had gone back to the castle, she scraped the earth off the faces of the bodies.'

'Wow!' said Lauren. 'That took some guts.'

'Young Ms Hayward is a very brave person,' agreed Gareth. 'When she saw it wasn't you, she phoned Sue Clark again and said she thought you must be locked up somewhere in there. She is someone it would be useful to have on our side. I think there's a future for her in our organisation.'

'And, after the phone calls, I assume Sue Clark swung into action,' said Lauren. 'Those special forces soldiers who turned up to rescue us.'

'Pierce Randall have some expert resources at their disposal, including their own private SWAT teams,' said Gareth. 'It was a Pierce Randall team who rescued us. And, as I'm sure you realised, once we were free I got them to alert our own people and told them to go to Laker Heath and deal with Guy.'

'They arrived just in time,' said Jake. He added, 'They killed him.'

'What would you have preferred?' asked Gareth. 'We could have locked him up, but sooner or later some smart lawyer would have got him released, and then he would have been a very serious and dangerous problem once more.'

'I saw The Index,' said Jake. 'It was in the hangar at Laker Heath.'

'Really?' said Gareth in a dry tone.

'How long has it been there?'

241

'I'm not really able to disclose any information regarding The Index,' said Gareth, 'but let's just say our people were ahead of you.'

'So why didn't you take the *Journal* at the same time? That was at the chapel as well.'

'The *Journal of the Order of Malichea* is of little interest. The Index is what people are after.'

'If you've had The Index all this time, then you know where all the books are hidden,' said Lauren accusingly. 'So why all that business, for so long, of following us around and seeing if we found any of the books?'

'To stop you, of course,' said Gareth. 'And, if you did find any, to take them off you. The books have to stay hidden for the common good.'

'You haven't thought of recovering them all and stashing them in that hangar at Laker Heath, along with the others you've got there?' asked Jake.

'Jake, there are hundreds and hundreds of them!' said Gareth. 'Many of them are safe where they are, spread far and wide, hidden, and protected by the Watchers. That way they stay safe. And with a helping hand from MI5.'

# Chapter 30

Jake and Lauren were driven back to their flat by Gerald. As they arrived, he told them, 'Don't worry, your flat is quite safe.'

'You've been inside it?' queried Lauren.

'Some of our people did a scan of it,' said Gerald. 'They haven't interfered with anything, I can assure you, we were just making sure no one had left any nasty surprises for you.'

With that he drove off. Jake looked towards their flat.

'Think we can take his word for it?' he asked.

'Yes,' said Lauren. 'With Guy dead and those kids locked up, I think we can say we're safe.'

'We've thought that before, and were wrong,' pointed out Jake.

'But The Index and the *Journal* have been found and are in a secure facility. Once everyone knows that, the game's over.'

'No it's not,' said Jake. 'The books are out there, still hidden. And now that Pierce Randall know where The Index is . . .'

'You think Gareth told Sue Clark?' asked Lauren.

'No, but it's a lead, isn't it? And the only one that we've got,' said Jake. 'Which means Pierce Randall will be pulling every string and pushing every button they can to get their hands on it.' He shook his head. 'It's not over. It'll never be over.'

As they walked along the pathway towards the block of flats, Jake's gaze caught their parked Mini Cooper. The side panel in the bodywork was still dented, the headlight was still broken. Lauren saw the gloomy expression on his face.

'Maybe now we'll have time to get it fixed,' said Lauren.

'I was just thinking that there's another thing we need to fix,' said Jake. 'Someone we need to thank.'

This time they drove to the caravan park on the outskirts of Sevenoaks. They'd phoned ahead to Dan to make sure that he and Gemma would be in for their visit. Gemma opened the door of the caravan to them. Dan was making coffee.

'We wanted to come and say thank you,' said Lauren to Gemma, as they walked in and sat down. 'If it hadn't been for you, we'd have been dead.'

'I know.' Gemma nodded.

'We heard what you did, scraping the dirt off the bodies,' said Jake. 'That took massive courage.'

'I had to find out if Dan had been killed,' said Gemma.

'I nearly was,' said Dan ruefully, bringing a tray with coffees on it and putting it on the low table.

'MI5 were really impressed,' said Jake. 'We hear they might be offering you a job.' He grinned. 'Though I guess that could be an official secret.'

Gemma shook her head.

'I'm not taking it,' she said. She smiled. 'I'm going into private practice. There's more money in it than working for the government.'

'Private practice?' queried Lauren.

'Pierce Randall,' said Gemma. 'They've offered me an internship.' She leant forward, an expression of triumph on her face. 'Sue Clark told me I could earn a million a year working for them. A million a year!'

'Yes,' said Jake. 'I expect you can.'

'One day I'll be able to buy Mum and Dan a proper home,' added Gemma. She gestured around the interior of the caravan. 'No more caravan park for them. And me, I'm moving into a flat in London, in the same block as Sue Clark. It's a very expensive place. Very smart!'

'Brilliant,' said Lauren, throwing a worried look Jake's way.

\*       \*       \*

As Jake and Lauren drove away from the caravan park, Jake at the wheel, he said, 'I think that Gemma will fit in very nicely at Pierce Randall.'

'In fact, I bet in a few years she'll be after Sue Clark's job,' added Lauren. 'She's very ambitious. Just the right person for Pierce Randall. What about us?' asked Lauren.

Jake laughed.

'I don't think we're Pierce Randall people at all,' he said.

'I mean, what happens next?'

'About the Malichea books, you mean?'

'Yes.'

'That depends,' said Jake. 'You always said your aim was to get that scientific knowledge out into the public arena. Use it to save lives.'

'But most people seem to want to use it as weapons, or to make money,' sighed Lauren. 'Maybe I was wrong and Gareth was right. Perhaps it's better for the books to stay hidden.'

'Who knows?' Jake shrugged. 'Maybe?' Then he grinned. 'Or maybe not,' he added and gave a sly chuckle. 'Maybe that's up to us.'

The world's greatest secrets are in danger of
falling into the wrong hands. It's down to renegades
Jake and Lauren to find them . . . before it's too late.

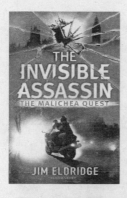

Read the WHOLE series

OUT NOW

Mosi is hiding his past. Patrick must find out why.
But the truth is dark . . . Two boys. Two lives.
One fight for survival.

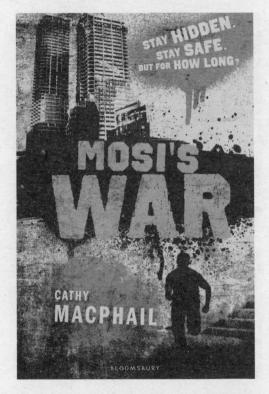

'Anything by Cathy MacPhail is unputdownable'
Julia Donaldson, *Guardian*

OUT NOW